THE
ATLANTROPA
ARTICLES

THE ATLANTROPA ARTICLES

A Novel

Cody Franklin

Mango Publishing

CORAL GABLES

For permission requests, please contact the publisher at:

Mango Publishing Group
2850 Douglas Road, 3rd Floor
Coral Gables, FL 33134 USA
info@mango.bz

For special orders, quantity sales, course adoptions and corporate sales, please email the publisher at sales@mango.bz. For trade and wholesale sales, please contact Ingram Publisher Services at customer.service@ingramcontent.com or +1.800.509.4887.

The Atlantropa Articles: A Novel
Library of Congress Cataloging
ISBN: (print) 978-1-63353-835-1 (ebook) 978-1-63353-836-8

Library of Congress Control Number: 2018956711

BISAC category code: FIC032000 FICTION / War & Military

Printed in the United States of America

Dedicated to my mother, Julie, without whose encouragement and support, my creative endeavors never would have begun.

Table of Contents

THE WESTERN KILN

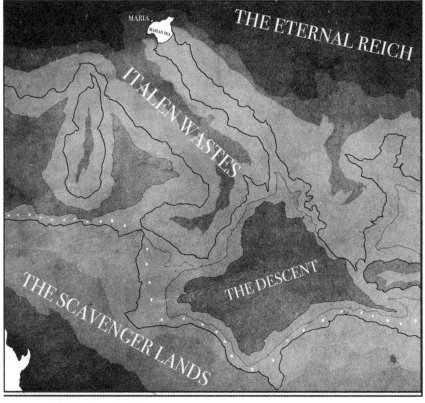

The Rusted Arm

What an absolute waste. Such a fine drink was now spilt onto the floor, mixing together with an ever-growing pool of blood from a Marian whore. Imagine that whiskey's journey. The time and effort it must have taken to reach perfection. Brewed and bottled, then put into a crate and transported all the way south to the edge of civilization...simply to be ruined in such a callous manner. It was an expensive bottle, and I'm certain the price matched the work. I was quite looking forward to enjoying such handiwork. Yet instead, all of it is now a puddle of glass and blood at my feet.

Dumb bitch.

I sit here in this booth waiting for somebody to settle the matter. Few patrons in the bar glance over, and those who do quickly turn back to their drinks. An injured bar-whore on this ferry is not a tragedy to warrant more than a few seconds of curiosity.

She will just not stop shrieking. The shaking mess is curled up next to the table she clumsily knocked over. She's wailing like a banshee, and it's getting on my nerves; her good hand is clutching the Reichsmarks that she stole from my pocket.

She had sat on my lap, slipped her hand in my pocket, and taken the money inside, thinking I wouldn't catch it. As she gripped the money, I in turn gripped her twig of a forearm and shattered that fucking thing in half. Bone is piercing out of the flesh, some red pulp is dripping onto the wooden floor...serves her right. She tried to get away and toppled everything over with her. The table...the drink...my patience.

A dark, cardinal-red river is flowing down her pale, fair skin. I was very eager to get acquainted with that body before we made landfall. She seemed like a quality girl. Blonde, an abundance of curves, smooth pearly skin. If she had made some good life decisions and weren't a bar-whore, I figure she could have made a fine Aryan wife. Just my luck the best looking specimen tries to be a thief. Pity.

I motion for another drink and for somebody to take this whimpering mess away from me. Four girls scurry into the bar.

One hands me a new bottle of liquor, the second places a mat over the pool of blood, and the last two drag away the sobbing bitch. It was a nice little display.

One of the girls snatches my Reichsmarks back from the bleeding bar-whore's grasp and places the money firmly into my hands. As the rest leave the room, she gives a gracious bow, apologizes in a regretful tone for the inconvenience, and finally floats out of the room to leave me in peace.

"What was that for?" a voice calmly says at the other end of the bar.

I turn to face its owner. His slim figure is draped in an overcoat that flows down to his knees. On top of an already bulky coat is a shell of metal-armored plates. They are golden, just like his features. Blond hair slicked back, with a short-trimmed beard to match. His youth of twenty years really contrasts with my own aging exterior. Even though we are only ten years apart in age, I can't help but notice the difference.

"You saw what she did, Ulric," I say, pointing to the mat which had been laid down to cover the puddle of blood. "Had to protect my money."

Ulric makes his way across the bar toward me, setting his attention on the still sideways table.

"Problems are settled differently down here," I explain to him in a collected manner, as we both prop the table back up.

"Quite different than Germania, I guess," Ulric hesitantly rationalizes, as he joins me at the booth. His voice is laced with nervousness. I expected he'd be a little uneasy, considering this is his first deployment down south. My brother has lived a quiet life in the pristine capital of the Reich. A place of beautiful monuments, tall winding towers, and dense green forests.

"Sometimes I don't know the strength of this thing," I say, shifting to display my left arm, or what is *now* my arm. Drops of the girl's blood paint the side of my rusted mechanical limb. I probably should wipe that off.

It's common practice to put artificial skin over such a thing, but I just never bothered. Fake skin never wrinkles: it stays in the same perfect condition forever, unlike the rest of me. I've already seen my skin age and wrinkle, even if it was just a bit. At least as the metal rusts, my body degeneration will be a uniform and balanced process.

I take a napkin and begin cleaning the blood off of my limb. I don't get why this arm is always the dominant one. Even ten years after losing it, it still thinks it's in charge.

"Don't you think there could have been another way handling that situation?" Ulric says, while watching the cleaning display. "Could have just stopped her and got the money back. She was just a little thing."

I nod in aloof agreement while cleaning away the last bits of blood. It was the same dark crimson as Ulric's uniform—standard for an S.S. Knight. The gold eagle and skull pinned to his chest shines against the lamp hanging above us.

"I wouldn't get caught up on it, Ulric. It's not like it was that much of a loss," I reason. "If you knew how many girls go through every season, you'd know she can be replaced like *that*." I snap my fingers, "Don't get queasy. I know you're a pacifist and all...."

"I'm not a pacifist," Ulric defends. "I just have never seen violence like that before."

"Not a pacifist, sure," I joke, pointing to his uniform.

"The Knighthood maintains cultural integrity," Ulric explains, his hands clenched together as his body slouches over. "We aren't some peace organization."

"So getting caught up on a bar-whore is maintaining culture?" I laugh, looking around the dim room. Not one of the occupants was looking back at us. The bartender was cleaning one of his glasses, having a quiet conversation with a man in a grey uniform. None pay much mind to my brother and me.

Ulric's eyes lock on the last drops of blood I am wiping from my limb. It's as if he has something to say, but instead he simply lets out a deep breath, unclenches his hands, and orders another drink.

"The Knighthood is about protecting the tribe," he explains.

"The only way to protect the tribe is to make sure we aren't attacked by another tribe," I state.

"There are many ways to protect a tribe, Ansel," Ulric lectures, his eyes narrowing, "such as respecting your fellow Aryans."

I chuckle to myself, almost spitting up my drink. Ulric wrinkles his brow at me with an expression of annoyance.

"Are you saying that I should have respected that whore just because she's an Aryan?" I choke out through spats of laughter.

"A tribe that fights amongst itself is bound to collapse," he concludes.

"We're not going to fight some great war just because I broke a thief's arm," I say. "If anything, you should be lecturing her for stealing."

Ulric slouches down into his seat. His hand loosely grips the handle of his pint.

"That woman was still an Aryan."

"That woman was still a thief," I say, taking a large gulp from my new whiskey.

We sit by a small window that overlooks the sea. A faint rumble permeates the walls as waves splash against the ferry. It always surprises me just how loud the sea is—a thousand little movements working in sync to create that recognizable hum. It's a rhythm in tune to the slow churn of the ship's engine.

This ferry isn't larger than the ships of the Kiln, but it's still impressive...for a water vessel. I'm surprised at how it can even stay afloat. It doesn't need wheels, treads, or magnets to grip onto the water. This is, by all means, a chunk of metal floating on top of a liquid surface. Mechanical feet were always something inherently genetic to the European.

For its remarkable size, there is barely a soul on this ferry. The only travelers I see are the standard bunch of sailors on their way south to the Kiln. Whores strut across the bar, but even they are few and far between; granted, that probably is because of me.

The Reich officially outlaws prostitution but down south, they turn a blind eye. Sailors had to be kept happy somehow in this remote edge of civilization.

I figure that if this region were run with the moral code of Germania up north, then no sailors would want to ship cargo. In the summer months when the heat is an issue, hell, I guarantee half of the ships would be abandoned and never leave port.

This time of year, the pay is doubled, eyes are turned away, and the sailors are kept happy with women before they embark on their long journeys ahead. There's a common saying here: "As long as the cargo ships and the Nests stay fertile, the Reich will always remain Eternal."

I can still make out, on the horizon, the towers of Maria peeking out from behind a cloud of dust and smoke. Unlike the capital of Germania or the city of London, there was no real organized design to Maria. The streets are narrow and winding; the towers, plopped everywhere...and the people are just as disorganized as the layout.

Yet it had the right location to serve as a port city, and in that regard Maria did its job.

"I don't want to mess this up," Ulric says, after a long silence. I look at him, his posture defeated and his head held low. The armor swallowed up his skinny figure.

"You won't mess up." I comfort him, lowering my pint glass. Our vessel is just shipping containers to some Eagle Nests down south and if we run into any enemy vessels, our ship will blast them before we even need help.

"But if I need to call in a Drop—" Ulric sputters out.

"You won't need to," I cut in.

"Alright. I'm just saying if I need to, if we're in a lot of danger—"

"You're nervous...I get it," I explain. "If we really need it I'll let you know, but only when I let you know."

Every ship that goes out into the Kiln is Reich property. That means that if a ship comes under attack by Scavengers and is about to go down, then the last-ditch effort is called in. An "Aegir" Drop—an orbital strike which drops a hunk of metal, crashing down onto the enemy like a meteor. Even though the Reich doesn't expand across Asia, it still expands into space. Space is more useful anyway. Only one kind of person is really trusted to use Aegir Drops responsibly—an S.S. Knight. Guess the Reich leaders don't have much faith in their sailors. I don't really blame them, considering the crewmen I've run into over the years.

Ulric, being a newly dubbed Knight, is taking his first maiden voyage into a new life. Calling in these Drops to protect the ships. That's why I invited my skittish brother to join my ship, so he can have a quality first experience. Well, that and it's the law.

"Why do you not want me to call in a Drop?" Ulric asks, his face contorting in confusion.

I look out the small window toward the swirling waves. My own battered reflection peers back at me. Sullen eyes, a few scars across my face, a shaggy beard. Years out in this place have certainly taken their toll on my body.

"It's cowardly," I say, in a dull dismissive tone, taking another drink.

Ulric perks himself up at the sound, confounded at what he just heard.

"Cowardly?!" he repeats in astonishment. "How is a weapon designed to save the lives of your men cowardly?" His voice lines with a twinge of hysteria.

I keep myself composed, looking back toward the window and my own battered face.

"My men don't need some orbital blast to save them," I explain in a hushed tone. "We have all the weapons we need on the ship. I prefer to get up close to the enemy."

"It isn't about what you prefer," Ulric explains. "It's policy by the Reich. A Knight needs to be on the ship no matter what...just in case."

"And I can disagree with Reich policies." I argue back, in a calm demeanor. This seems to get Ulric even more infuriated. "I'm still allowing a Knight to come onto the ship. It's just we won't really need your services."

"Why did I even come on this journey with you then if I can't even do anything?" he asks, his eyes wide.

"Think of it like an introduction into life in the Kiln. You learn how things are done."

"I've learned for four years in school, Ansel," Ulric complains, his eyes lowered toward his half-empty pint.

"They are two different beasts," I say, taking another swig. "You think I knew anything about the Kiln until I joined the military? Every man thinks he knows everything at your age, until they don't."

Jokingly, I flex my metallic arm. My mind flashes back to an earlier time. I was Ulric's age, and it too was my first time in the Kiln. Yet my reason for arriving was far different. Eagle Nest #15 had been invaded by Scavengers. A gun was placed in my hand and I was told to storm those large, tall towers. "Take back the Nest," they said, and I followed.

Took shrapnel to the torso. Everything went black. Within a day though, I was back in the fight with a new mechanical arm, and able to avenge that limb along with those innocent civilians murdered. Wasted many revolver rounds, firing into the surrendering Scavengers' skulls.

A soft female voice rings out across the bar from speakers in the ceiling.

"Attention all passengers. We shall be arriving at the Edge in ten minutes. If you have not done so, get to your belongings and prepare to disembark the ferry when the time comes."

I lift myself up with a heavy grunt. My metallic limb clangs as the mechanisms inside spin to support my weight. Ulric silently stands up alongside me. His face is still sullen with disappointment.

"No matter how much reading you do," I reason to him, pointing a hand on his shoulder, "there is nothing that really prepares a man to life in the Kiln other than being in the Kiln."

"I...I know," he says, with a trailing voice. "I was just expecting to do something."

"And you will, eventually. Just for now, be appreciative that you get a crash course in how things are down here."

We pick up the small duffle bags we brought along on our journey. There wasn't much that I packed. Anything of particular use up north was pointless down south. Most of my gear minus my armor, which I was already wearing, was on my ship anyway.

Ulric and I stand at the side of the ferry, gripping onto the railing overlooking the sea. This water always had a strange pungent smell to it. It smells of dead fish, but there hasn't been a single fish in this small sea for centuries. With every movement of each wave, that foul odor splashes against the ship.

The occupants of the boat go about their business, preparing to dock. Some wear metal-plated armor, just like my brother and I. Others wear simple, grey uniforms. Ulric holds himself stiff as a board, cautious to stay out of the way of everyone.

In the distance, I can see a large orange cloud wafting over the horizon. It is like a monster slowly revealing its presence. A fog clashing with the teal, rippling waves. We are getting close to the Edge.

"What is that?" Ulric asks, pointing to the orange fog.

"That, Ulric—" I explain in a matter-of-fact manner, "—that is a dust storm. We're getting close now."

After a few minutes, the concrete world of the Edge comes into full view. Our boat slows itself down as it navigates past the traffic of other ferries and vessels, each either docking or leaving.

The flow of bodies bustles around the city like an ant colony against the gargantuan stone towers and majestic statues, the largest of which is a statue of gold in the image of a man in a flowing overcoat. One arm seems to touch the orange sky as the other rests on a large stone tablet. By his side is a pole with an eagle, its wings outstretched. This statue seems to have the most people crowded around it, all wishing to get a look at one of the Reich's main heroes.

The ferry blows its horn to announce its arrival at the concrete shore and the crowd begins disembarking. A long, narrow bridge slowly moves toward solid ground, allowing the flood of people to spew forth from the vessel. Ulric and I navigate our way through a crowd of sailors, crewmen, and whores, all going to their own destination. As all depart and disappear into the sea of people, we both stop and stare at the sight in front of us.

These buildings must be thousands of years old and yet there is hardly a crack on them, only an orange hue which has caked itself onto the façades of these structures. They are all ornate. Carved with pictures of events from the past. Armored warriors defending against an unstoppable wave. A pact between two men holding up a single document.

Above these structures loom great statues, which remain as pristine as the day they were first constructed. Images dedicated to Führers of the past, Reich heroes who fought in the Kiln, or even depictions of eagles. In every area of the Edge, red-and-gold flags wave
about, gloriously.

It truly is a magnificent sight; however, it isn't the sight that I have come for.

We stroll through the crowd. Sailors bumble past us on their way to their designated ships. Guards in their large metal suits lumber by with a metallic clank at every footstep. Smaller soldiers march about, waiting to be loaded onto a ship destined for some Eagle Nest out in the Kiln.

As the minutes roll past, we move away from the pungent odor of the sea. The sound of the waves crashing against the Edge disappears in the noise of the human traffic. With every step, dust becomes more prevalent on the white, ancient floor. Wind begins to howl and cry as hot, dry air overtakes the smell of the sea.

There is no horizon in front of me. Instead, the blue sky simply meets a small white barrier. It's a wall that goes up to my waist. On this wall is a line of flagpoles, each flying the flag of the Eternal Reich, a swastika emblazoned on each and every one. This simple wall is the only thing preventing onlookers from tumbling down into the world below.

After about ten minutes of navigation, we've made our way to the literal edge of this concrete place. As I look down past the white barrier caked in sand, I can see the desert world that stretches endlessly onward. It is the edge of the great concrete dam that holds in the entire sea which we have just traversed by ferry.

I look down the curved face of a structure that has remained stable and intact since the days of the first Aryans. This dam is the arrival point for most people traveling into the vast desert beyond.

Through the rippling desert air, I locate the vast array of ships lined in a row against the dam's edge. Those are the true docks. Each ship packed with special cargo, preparing to sail forthright into the vast expanse of desert and salt.

From the bottom docks onward, there is nothing more than endless rolling hills of orange desert. I take in the sight of ships curving over the dunes. Going off into the horizon. Long strings of dusty clouds trail behind them as their treads slowly carry them south into the basin beyond.

"Welcome to the Kiln," I mutter to my brother, reaching out a hand to the magnificent sight.

"It sure is different than how I pictured it," Ulric remarks, peering over with me, "It's far more...arid."

"Well, it is a desert," I laugh. "What did you expect?"

"I don't know what I expected.... So, which ship is yours?" Ulric asks, gesturing a hand toward the ships lined against the dam far below.

I point to the largest of the hulking masses of steel. "There she is, there's the *Howling Dark*."

"She's quite a big one," Ulric remarks.

"Well there's a reason we've never needed to call in the Drop," I say.

We stay there for a while, simply gazing out into the orange expanse of sea. After that, we turn around and head to the statue that has loomed over us since we first arrived at the Docks. Its façade has been worn down by centuries of dust and sand, but that didn't stop it from being magnificent.

I look up upon the calm statue that for centuries has looked off into that endless desert world. Sharp cheekbones define a strong, handsome face. It has wavy hair, similar to that of the ancient Greeks. Its tall body is draped in garments and chains, yet still remains composed. One hand points toward the sky, as another clasps onto the documents that created all the dams of Atlantropa.

We were always taught that he was truly the perfect, ideal Aryan. The man who started our entire race. Standing here underneath this statue, I can't help but feel a warmth inside my heart. It simply gives off the aura of a father, like he is looking down at his people who are prospering.

"What do you think he would have thought of this?" Ulric asks me.

I squint and wrinkle my brow to get a clearer view of the statue's face. I take in the meticulous details of the robes. Every inch tells a story through a series of symbols and images about the people of Europe. It is a story that culminates in the Reich and the rise of the Aryans. The people.

"I don't know how much he would think of large statues of himself," I reply.

"I mean, what do you think he would have thought about this desert? You think he would have still gone through with constructing the dams if he knew the sea would just become one large desert?"

My eyebrows rise, and I look back down to Ulric, his face still turned upward.

"I assume so," I guess, not really knowing much of what he would have wanted. "Peace was assured, everyone came together. So it worked out," I reply, gazing up once more.

We then look to the stone engraving that stands at the base of the statue. It's a mural of two men, the one in the statue and another man, the Architect, both grasping a stone tablet with one hand. Rays radiate from the stone as a group of men look on in the background. On the stone is a single phrase: "The Atlantropa Articles."

Underneath the depiction of the two men is a short poem, engraved onto the marble:

> *I light my path with the flame of reason,*
> *I warm my heart with the pride of race,*
> *I love my Führer for all Eternal,*
> *For his life is what gave me grace.*
>
> *In Memoriam to the Eternal Führer Adolf Hitler*
> *(1889–1939)*

"He'd be proud that a kid is so ambitious about his message," I say to Ulric, his eyes analyzing the poem before us.

"You really think so?" Ulric asks with a smile.

"Of course," I reply, smiling back. "Sieg Heil."

"Sieg Heil."

The Howling Dark

The dam scales across the desert like a towering cliff. Its sheer size makes it appear more like a natural formation than a manmade construction, as if the Reich had nothing to do with this dam and Earth had formed this cliffside herself. The journey down to the desert below is a long one, even in an elevator. I feel cramped inside this small metal box hugging the face of the dam on a slow descent into the Kiln.

Such a long journey leads my mind to wander. I imagine the sea that is behind me, all of the water held back only by a thick barrier of centuries-old concrete. If this dam weren't here, I'd be surrounded by whales and fish. Ships would be sailing above my head instead of below my feet. It's a strange concept to ponder.

Sunlight peeks in through a thin row of windows along the cabin's ceiling. In a slow meticulous fashion, rays of light from the setting sun crawl down the walls. White specks of sand glisten as they meet.

The sand that has collected on the cabin floor is tossed up with a jolt from the steel box. Millions of particles drift about the room like a swarm of tiny flies. Sand dyes the air a hue of lightish orange. It's as thick as liquid. If I weren't wearing a mask, I doubt I could even breathe.

As is policy, Ulric and I are wearing the appropriate breathing apparatus and are dressed in uniforms of metal and bright, red-and-gold cloth garments. We resemble knights prepared for battle more than men awaiting to sail.

Special fluid fills each and every garment we wear. It is all for cooling purposes. When the sea dried up, it left behind a basin. A basin of salt and sand that soaks in every bit of sunlight poured into it. Even in the safest conditions, the temperatures can be so high you'd die in a matter of hours, if not minutes.

The rumor always was the Sun could become so intense in this basin that the heat could melt even glass. From that generations-old belief, this place received its name: "The Kiln." The Kiln is the basin that the Mediterranean left behind. It's a bowl of salt, sand, and death.

We descend farther. With each moment we come closer to being level with the evening sun.

"How did you first feel when coming into the Kiln?" my brother asks in a stuttering voice, breaking a moment of relative silence.

I ponder for a second.

"In the military? No nerves. Just rushed right in," I state in a boastful tone. "First day as a Captain? Fuck, now that was nerve-racking. Thought I'd crash the ship on the first departure. Talk about daunting."

"Feels like I got a whirlpool in my stomach."

"Look, it gets easier after a while. The sand will become your old friend, and after being out there it won't seem so daunting anymore. I will admit, though, having a big enough gun helps."

"Just not too big." Ulric raises a finger.

"You're still on about the Aegir Drop?" I groan, turning to my brother, taking in his entire display of silver armor. His helmet is a jagged and sharp thing encompassing his usually gaunt face. Wrapped around his body is a series of light-brown scarves. Draped over his shoulder is a dark violet cape.

"Why do you not want me to do it?" he insists in a whine, looking back at me with two orange visors shining bright in this dusty dark box.

"I already told you." I abruptly spit, turning away from him, focusing my attention on the dust particles floating about.

"It's a tool at our disposal...that's all I'm saying." Ulric insists in a calmer voice, a bid to level for me to change my mind. Yet I know I will not change my mind.

"Not all tools need to be used," I say, raising my arms up. I begin pacing around what little space I can in here. "You get in a fight with an unarmed man, and you got a knife, sure you can use it, doesn't mean you aren't any less of a pussy."

"They are Scavengers, why do you care how you kill them. Think they'll judge you?" Ulric reasons, and to that I burst out in laughter.

"No," I say through chuckles, "I just don't want to judge myself. This is the Kiln, our domain. I shouldn't have to rely on anyone else, but me." I thump my rusted metal arm against my metallic armor. It gives off a satisfying clank with each beat.

Ulric turns away defeated, and we both face the empty wall. The sunlight continues its migration across the elevator as we go farther down the dam.

"Did Father ever have a chance to tell you the story about his time in the Italen Sands?" Ulric asks, breaking the slight lull in the conversation, "...when he was stationed there?"

I turn my head to face him. His identification number and name pop up on my display. A helmet in the Kiln is important for the days when the sun reflects off of the white salt, or when the desert kicks up a storm to ruin an afternoon.

"He's told me, bits and pieces but no specifics," I ponder, thinking back to the conversations I had with that stern man in my childhood. "Why? Did he tell you?"

"He told me before I went off to college." Ulric contemplates, preparing to dive deep into a story. "He talked about how his division was sent in to clear out squatters that occupied that abandoned city, Rome. Nobody knew why they chose to stay there...nothing but desert, you know. Sand dunes covered everywhere except this temple."

The elevator, after a few minutes of creeping, has finally leveled with the tops of the ships. I can make out the golden flag of the Reich flowing high atop one vessel.

"The squatters were starving in that temple. Dad said they didn't look like us. They had dark hair. Foreign features. They weren't dark like the Raiders, but not fair-skinned like Aryans. He figured they were the last remnants of the Romans."

The engines from the ships permeate the elevator cabin, throwing more sand into the air as the deep bassoon of a tremor ripples out. Ulric seems to be lost in thought.

"They were too stubborn to leave when their homeland dried up but had managed to keep fish alive, in these pools of water," he continues, his voice trailing.

The bustling docks come into full view as the elevator slows to a crawl.

"At least the fish had *once* been alive. See, they had so many people, they needed a lot of fish to feed everyone. It was the last water reserve they had, so space was limited. Well, it was too limited. Most of the fish had drowned."

"What?" I chuckle. "How does a fish drown in water?"

"Well, they need oxygen and there is only so much oxygen in water. If there are too many fish breathing that oxygen, then they can't breathe and suffocate," Ulric answers. "These Romans had too many people, not enough space, and couldn't keep the fish alive. So they starved."

"They don't seem like they were the smartest people," I scoff. "They should have left," I continue, wagging a finger.

"Yes they should have. But they were stubborn," Ulric concludes in that matter-of-fact, scholarly voice.

An armored Ulric, donned in a violet cloth, turns himself toward me as the elevator doors open, releasing a taste of the scalding heat, much like an oven. Even through my protective layer, the heat is still a presence.

"No matter how natural it is for a fish to be in water, there is always the possibility that it can drown," my brother concludes to me, his voice calm and full of purpose.

"That's a good story," I say to him, feeling the rippling heat of the Kiln scraping against my metal, "but this desert is big enough for all of us to breathe."

The cracked stone surface of the Docks is so thick with sand that each step we take leaves imprints from our metal boots. Everything down here—the elevator, the docks, and the ships— all appear to be dyed with the same orange powder. Sand is just something non-negotiable down here. Winds carries the stuff every day, and it makes cleaning anything a pretty pointless endeavor.

As we make our way down an orchestra of machinery, men, and cargo, I explain the sights to a bewildered Ulric. The dam, commonly just called the Marian Dam, towers over the entire display. Trains and carts speed across platforms constructed on its solid concrete face, stretching so long that it curves into the horizon.

For as impressive as the Marian Dam is, it is nothing compared to the biggest: the dam that keeps the entire Atlantic Ocean at bay. The pair of us stroll across the dock, leaping out of the way as cranes lift rusting containers and swing them far above like an acrobat.

Yet these cranes were tiny when compared to the hulking mechanical beasts to our left. Officially these machines with bows, sterns, and everything in between are simply called "ships." They are shaped like ships and they sail the desert like a ship would sail the sea.

In practice, these machines were much more like a tank. A tank that could successfully navigate across the ever-shifting waves of the Kiln. Every ship in the Kiln at one point was an actual watercraft, or that is how the rumor is told. The Kiln is a beacon which attracts such rumors.

Even if it were true, I doubt the ships in front of us look like they did before the sea dried up. To survive down here, all have been heavily modified with an assortment of metal plates and makeshift towers. Guns were removed and replaced with the modern weaponry of today. The treads. Oh my, the treads.

To the side of each ship were added gargantuan treads that allowed the machines to grip into the sandy ground and propel themselves forward.

Eventually I see her. The tall, jagged towers of cobbled-together steel peeking just above her neighbors. The *Howling Dark*. It's a shame we can't stay here during leave. Ever since I was assigned to this ship a decade ago, I have put my blood and sweat into making it the fiercest ship among the carriers. Looking at her is how I imagine a proud man feels after making a home for his family. I have no delusions of such a thing, so this...is my home.

The ship's wide stern is facing the docks. Behind it is a large steel crane, meticulously lifting a series of gigantic steel boxes right into the center of the vessel.

The *Howling Dark* casts a wide presence. For just one moment, I want to take in this full view of her majesty—one I rarely get out in the desert. Her elaborate stern reaches high into the desert air. Banners of red, gold, and silver drape over the side, each woven in with a swastika of the Reich.

Engraved into the metal work is the depiction of an eagle, its wings outstretched as it clutches onto a large broadsword. Wrapped around the sword is a long winding piece of parchment bearing the words: *For without the sacrifices of those before, I could not stand before you.*

Pieces of the engravement are missing, however, covered up in a patchwork of various metals that speckle her rusting shell. A testament of the numerous battles she has persevered. Even with the patchy metalwork, the intricate sculpting of Aryan heroes and legends on the back still filled me with a sense of awe. It's one of the few things that can do that to me anymore.

I lead Ulric to a makeshift contraption hanging at the back of the vessel. We clamber inside, and with a press of a button we are lifted up across the side of the boat. Noise from its bustling machinery begins to fade away as we are taken further and further up the ship's hull. The wind reveals itself as my helmet protects me from a blast of hot sand.

The lift ends its journey with a loud clang and we stop, having reached the deck. I'm met with the sight of a busy crew, fifty or so men, all dressed in armor like Ulric and I. Their capes are flowing in the desert wind; some have them tied around their waist so they aren't a nuisance. Each body goes about their small duty to make sure we are prepared to sail. Guns must be properly loaded. Flags must be unfurled. Engines must start.

As I slowly clamber off the lift the crew pauses their activities and turns their attention to me. My metal boots meet the steel of the ship in a loud clang. Every eye on the deck is on me as I straighten myself out and raise my voice.

"Hello, men." I boom. "This...is my brother, S.S. Knight Ulric Manafort. He is new to the Kiln, and will accompany us on our journey. It is his job to protect us on our journey, if need be, and for that you are to treat him with the utmost respect."

I turn to my brother, clasp my feet together, puff out my chest and salute him with one arm raised high.

"Sieg Heil," I bellow, followed by fifty other voices yelling in unison: "Sieg Heil!"

"Carry on," I order, waving them off to their own work, and the dock complies.

"Protection, huh?" Ulric comments in a curious voice lined with hopeful optimism.

"I'm required to say that," I mutter in a deadpan manner.

If the two large towers sprouting from the deck were trees, then their leaves would be the numerous banners that were strung atop them. Wire and cable dangling between the two appeared like vines in a jungle. Between the two trees was a series of arches, each pointed at the top. They just recently closed to encompass the steel boxes housed in the center of the ship.

"The closest tower to the bow houses the main bridge, while the second near the rear houses the defenses. Of course, most of the ship is covered in some form of weaponry for protection, but that tower is just, extra defenses," I explain to Ulric.

We navigate to the center of the ship, where the crates are being loaded in. As the crew hurries past us, my attention narrows in on one man with a small metal frame donned in a cloth of dark yellow. He is hunched over, analyzing a slab of metal in his hand. I don't think he has spotted us through the crowd. I wait and wait. Eventually, I clear my throat and he turns around, startled, apparently not noticing my presence.

"By the fucking Führer, don't scare me like that!" he exclaims. "When did you get here? Sneaking up behind me."

"This is the sixth time I've been able to do that, Volker," I say through spats of laughter, "You need to have more spatial awareness. I was yelling to the rest of the crew."

"Well, somebody has to account for all the crates. Guns, food, water, can't forget anything. Not to mention resources for ourselves," Volker defends himself in a high-pitched, grating voice. "Who is that?" he asks me, devoid of breath, pointing a gloved finger toward a puzzled Ulric.

"Volker, this is Ulric, my brother. He'll be the Knight on our trip," I explain in a light-hearted demeanor, still chuckling from the image of Volker's jumping body. "Ulric, this is First Officer Wilhelm Volker."

"Ah. The brother," Volker remarks in a reminiscent tone, extending his pointing hand toward Ulrich and offering him an open handshake. "He's told me a lot about you."

"Really?" Ulric says, shaking Volker's hand.

"Probably, I don't know, the words jumble together over time," Volker jokes. "But it's nice to meet you. Hopefully you're not too much like your brother." He nudges me a few times with his elbow, and I laugh in return.

"So what is the status on departure?" I ask him. Volker hands me the metal slab and I analyze through its data.

"It seems we have accounted for all of the shipments," Volker replies in a more logistical tone. "Most of these supplies are weapons, a few boxes are for food. We'll be ready for departure in a few hours."

"That works," I reply, looking down at the slab. "I'll just go around the ship and inspect everything, make sure it's all in working order."

"Sounds good," Volker replies, taking the slab back from me.

"What should I do?" Ulric asks in an uncertain voice.

"Come with me," I say. "If you're going to spend some time on this ship, you might as well get acquainted."

For the next few hours, Ulric and I wander around, inspecting every operation to make sure everything is in working order. The flags have been set. The weapons have been loaded. The treads have been cleaned. The crates have been secured. Even the engine room is now running, after I checked to see whether Keller finished drinking. By all accords, we are ready to set sail.

I stand on the tower closest to the bow, on a balcony right outside the main bridge. I can see everything, but for now I face the boundless sea before me. In the distance I spot an orange cloud floating over the horizon, stirred up by another ship. Out there, that will only be an ominous sign. The high winds shaping the grand dunes out there brush against my armor. I cling onto metal bars that have been stripped bare by the years of abuse from these conditions.

Looking down, I see a crowd awaiting my signal. I give a stiff-armed salute, and they respond in kind before rushing to their stations. With a slow walk, I wrap around the balcony to face the port and, with it, the mountain that is the dam.

I'm on the other side of the tower, and I see that the dock in our area has cleared out its people and machines in anticipation of our departure. I shouldn't keep them waiting. At the main deck in the center of the ship stands the last group of deckhands. They too look up at me, and I thrust out my arm rigid and true once again—in unison, they salute as well.

"Are we ready to depart, sir?" Volker cuts in.

"Yes, we are, all hands to stations," I reply.

"All hands to stations," Volker radios to the crew. Sirens blare, and the Dock beneath us begins to clear out. I can hear the yelling down below, as all brace for the ship to awaken.

"Start the engines," I say to Volker, and he repeats the command into his radio.

The Bridge rumbles like a volcano beneath our feet. Lights flicker and walls quake as black smoke funnels up the pipes and explodes upward in a triumphant roar. The *Howling Dark* has come alive.

"Take her away," I command, and it is done. A soft growl permeates the cabin. The treads awaken in a slow churn, grinding up the desert beneath. In response, an orange cloud rises from below as the ship creaks away from the concrete. I walk out of the bridge to view the cloud dissipate.

The ship hurls sand onto the concrete like a wave crashing against a stormy beach. Metal bars rattle as the ship picks up speed. Treads rotate like heavy steel clocks swirling about to bring us forward. She's a lumbering beast, and with another thunderous horn she signals that she is leaving port. I stroll back onto the Bridge and check the conditions. Everything is in working order. I stand there and watch as the ship leisurely cascades over its first sand dune of the journey. The banners tied to the front of the ship's bow catch a gust of wind. I take in how graciously they fly in the breeze—those red-and-gold flags, each emblazoned with a white swastika at the center, fluttering against a world of apricot sand.

Glasslands

The night is calm. The stars dazzle, as if the lights of Germania were above us. Cosmic clouds twirl around in a fashion similar to that of the dust kicked up by the ship's treads. We have passed the first area of sand dunes and have entered a small sea of salt—a flat plain of white crystal that is blinding during the day, but at night it is a different tale. The salt flats, when the sun goes down, transform into an endless mirror. A smooth surface so reflective one could shave while looking down.

We have sailed for three days, and our trip has only begun. The journey for ships is always long. Planes can always make supply drops to Eagle Nests in a fraction of the time, but there are far too many crates, and far too many Nests to be supplied for that to be reliably done. If it takes a couple of ships a couple weeks to make the journey, it's still worth it to the Reich.

To that, I have no complaints. Without the ships and the Kiln, I wouldn't have a job. I don't know if I could survive in the northern Reich, as much as I love the idea of it. Perhaps I love this ship because it's an escape. It's the only place that feels like home, even if I have to deal with the men on it. It's better than facing the perfection and the "proper" behavior for an Aryan man. Beating whores isn't considered civilized up there, as Ulric so delicately explained.

That's what I'd be like up north. I'd have to be like Ulric.

I look down from the tower onto a series of campfires scattered across the deck. It was large enough, and metal enough, that nobody had to worry about the fire spreading. Groups are huddled about, laughing at stories and drinking. At this time of night, there is not much to do otherwise. The course has been set, the journey is long, and the computer does most of the automated navigation. Why I am still on the Bridge, I don't know.

Very few actually stay on the Bridge. Usually it's just Volker, myself, and the Second Officer, a timid young kid called Witzel. I'd say he's about Ulric's age. We're the only two in the Bridge. I lean against the navigational dashboard, looking at the crowd below while Witzel stands in an upright posture, hands at his back, examining the charts on the wall.

"We're still going in the right direction, Witzel," I joke, taking a swig from my whiskey flask. Oftentimes the night can be long, and a few shots of liquor can help. Witzel swirls around uncomfortably, his hands still tied behind his back.

"I know, sir," he sputters out in a rash, quiet voice, "I just like double checking."

My response to this is a series of agreeable grunts as I straighten out my back. My hands rummage through the pouch on my chest and I pull out another cigar. The armor I wear is covered in a series of pouches for any occasion. Pockets for cigars, whiskey, water, bullets, all strewn across my waist and chest.

"Do you smoke, Witzel?" I ask with a casual mutter, reaching a cigar out toward the awkward lad.

"No, sir," he replies, "I never really got into it."

"It grows on you down here. This is only your...what? Second year?"

"Yes sir."

"You got time."

The large metal door swings open with a low creak. Footsteps signify that somebody is entering the Bridge. I swivel my head around and spot Volker. Without the helmet, he sports a buzzed head of sandy blond hair. His nose is more pointed compared to most, but it doesn't curve like a Scavenger's.

"Everything seem to be under control, Captain?" he asks in a raspy voice, placing his helmet onto a table adjacent to the door.

"Well, we haven't fallen into a canyon yet, so I say everything is alright." I mutter, continuing to puff on the cigar. Smoke floats gently up into the dimly lit ceiling. The room has very few lights.

I can turn on more lights if need be, but I like the darkness for now. Things are already so bright during the day. This can be a break. The smoke from the cigar absorbs the colors of orange and blue from the navigational screens and buttons on the dashboard, which offer most of the illumination in this room.

"Something could have popped over the horizon in the span of a walk around the ship," Volker jokes, making his way across the Bridge, his boots clanging against the ground. A low hum permeates the cabin—a reminder of the engines underneath doing their work to keep the treads moving. Even with the relatively thick walls of the ship, the desert wind is still present, gently whistling as it rubs against the windows and steel.

"We've just left Maria, you know there're no Scavenger ships this far north. You're becoming paranoid, Volker," I remark. "Cigar?" I suggest, handing him a finely rolled up piece of tobacco. "Witzel wasn't very interested."

"His loss," Volker jokes, accepting the second cigar from me. Witzel turns around for a brief moment, a blank look in his eyes before turning back toward the chart. How long does it take to analyze such a thing? Probably just looking at it to avoid conversation.

"Not like we get many chances to smoke anyway," I say, holding the cigar between my fingers. The campfires flicker down below, as shadowed bodies stumble their way about past the various guns welded to the deck.

"Wife doesn't like me smoking," Volker complains, releasing a cloud of smoke. It goes past his shallow eyes; bags have made their home underneath the sockets, a legacy of stressful days in this place.

"Wife probably doesn't like you going over for months at a time into this hot cauldron, but here we are," I say with a smirk.

We both stand in silence for a brief moment, holding onto our cigars, looking out into the vast expanse. The outside winds batter against the walls.

"Hear the attacks are getting worse out on the border near Africa?" he explains, pointing off into some unknown target in the distance. "Some Nests even had their defenses overrun. Had to call in the Drops to even get them to scatter."

"Where'd you hear that?" I ask.

"Just rumors."

"Everything is rumors," I mutter, while finishing off whatever whiskey was left in my flask. Damn.

"Rumors are the newscasts of the desert, Captain," Volker sneers, as more smoke trails past his jagged face.

I raise the empty flask in mild agreement to his words. Scavenger attacks have been something that the Reich has dealt with ever since the Reclamation. The Eternal Führer banished them from the Continent, and ever since they've wanted nothing more than to get back inside.

"That one Scavenger vessel two years ago, remember that?" Volker reminisces with a grin, "Fucking thing flared and gave away its position, *then* tried to lob rounds at us before we even reached the range of their guns!"

"And the damn shots landed a hundred meters from our ship," I say. "Gave their position away and we could just blow them up." My hands whip into the air to illustrate the ship combusting from our artillery shots. Volker's wide smirk slowly devolves into an emotionless face before taking another swig.

"Where do you think they go?" Volker asks in a somber inflection.

"Where do they go?" I repeat in puzzlement, attempting to process the question.

"Like, do they just park those ships in caves or something. Do they live in cities? What causes a people to just hop on machines and try to pillage innocents? You ever think of that?"

I never actually have. Does somebody need to question why the sun beats down on the desert? Or why a storm can destroy all in its path. It is just nature.

"Just figured it's how they were. We have loot and they want it. It's that simple," I conclude, walking toward a cupboard, opening it, and revealing a bottle of whiskey among its contents. "Do flies need a reason to seek honey? No, they simply buzz toward it and get stuck. Maybe that was the burden we carried, attracting the flies."

Volker agrees with a grunt and takes another puff.

"If I was on the other side of the Reich border I know that would be all I'd want to do," Volker comments.

My attention turns back to the huddled groups down below. I hear the cheers and songs rising like the smoke from fires.

"What do you think they're talking about down there?" I ask, pointing to the orange lights scattered upon the deck.

"Usual stuff. What Nests we're going to. What they'll do when we reach them. What they did on their leave," Volker lists off in a dull fashion.

"That would be a quick conversation. Most probably went and whored around, got drunk, then came back," I reply.

"Speaking from experience, Captain?" Volker teases. To this I laugh and raise my bottle another time.

The engine buzz carries on like a constant rhythmic hum. Like a low voice chanting out. Wait. No, those actually are voices. Music gently rises from the deck, along with the noise of the drinking men. There are more sounds however. An odd, distant and fuzzy chanting.

> Raise the flag! The ranks tightly closed!
> The SA march with quiet, steady step.

"Odd song," I state to Volker, taking one last drag from my cigar. "Ever heard that before?"

"Nah," Volker denies. "How did they even get a sound system onto the deck?"

Putting out the cigar bud, I walk toward the door, tossing the wasted cigar into a rubbish bin. "I'll go investigate," I announce to Volker, before opening the door and exiting the Bridge.

The door leads to an indoor staircase that descends down the tower. The creaking of the ship is always the most prevalent here. Sometimes it sounds like the wires and metal plating that hold this tower together will break apart at just a strong breeze. During the day, with the sun beaming down and temperatures up, I'd need to wear a helmet, but at night, when the moon is out, there is no need.

Opening the door, I pace slowly onto the metallic deck. Ashes and sparks dance about the ship as the soft Kiln wind carries them away. The crew have divided themselves into various campfires with six or seven crowded around a flame. Some men are singing, some are brawling. Most are drunk.

> *Comrades shot by the Red Front and reactionaries*
> *March in spirit within our ranks.*

The song of trumpets and chants is coming from a group considerably louder than all the others near the bowsprit. While making my way over, a few of the men notice my armor and immediately stand a little straighter. The larger, bronze-colored armored one with a shaved bald head is standing above them all, knee raised up, arms outstretched in theatrical display at the story he is telling.

"And the fucker came up to me and said, 'If you talk to me like that one more time...' and it was right there when I knocked him onto the ground. I don't like knives you see, gotta just—"

He wrestles with the air, pretending to down a figurative man. The crowd's attention has now turned to me placing myself on a chair, joining the group bunched around the flames. The air becomes thick with nervousness. They aren't used to the Captain himself joining them in their drinking.

"After I stopped throttling his neck, he eventually regained consciousness but you should have *seen* the wedding party—" he pauses, as his good eye slowly turns to meet mine.

"That's a good story you should continue," I encourage.

After a few seconds of wide-eyed befuddlement, the man quickly regains his composure and waves his arm down to the fire. "Welcome to our humble fire, Captain," he says with a smile half full of teeth.

> *Clear the streets for the brown battalions,*
> *Clear the streets for the storm division!*

The muffled voices continue to sing and I turn my attention to the small wooden box that is blaring the music. It's cobbled together in a makeshift fashion with screws and tape. With every call of the horns it rumbles like it will burst open at any moment.

"That's an odd contraption," I remark, pointing at the box. "Where did you get it?"

"He made it himself," a man to my right says in a slurred tone. I can't place his name, but he appears to be a guard by his uniform. More armor, more pouches, and a rifle by his side. Each ship in the Kiln was assigned at least a few still-active military members, although most of the men who sail in the Kiln have themselves at one time served in the Kiln.

"Thank you, but I would like to hear from Chief Engineer Keller," I calmly reply, my eyes turning toward a face covered in a fix of dust and grease.

"I did make this myself, Captain," Keller beams, pointing to the box. He stops the song, and the group bemoans their loss of entertainment. With one quick fashion he opens up the wooden lid and takes out a dark and round, yet flat disc. "A friend of mine sold it to me in Eagle Nest #18. Said some Scavengers found it while scouring the desert."

"Scavenging is illegal, you realize," I state, leaning back.

Keller's eyes freeze for a fraction of a second, still grasping at the disc. The fire reflects speckles of orange off of the disc's glossy coating. I can tell his mind is churning with the right words to say.

"Technically, yes it is, but I didn't scavenge this, somebody else did," Keller defends.

"Fair enough," I respond, not caring much that the disc was actually found. I've never agreed much with the rules about scavenging in the Kiln. It's a vast desert. I'm sure there are things out here worth some money. Yet the law demands that nobody take even a trinket from the sands. The reason for this is unclear. Some argue that it's to prevent some ancient virus from resurfacing to plague humanity once again. Or maybe, the Scavengers planted a lie in the desert. I doubt the latter, I don't think the Scavengers are smart enough to even replicate an Aryan artifact.

Keller takes the disc and places it neatly back into the box. With a closing of the lid and the press of a button the song continues on with its jubilant melody.

> *Millions are looking upon the swastika full of hope,*
> *The day of freedom and of bread dawns!*

The voices ringing from the box were muffled and distant. Perhaps it was just the rudimentary nature of Keller's design, but this song certainly didn't sound like anything I'd heard before. It sounded...old. Like singing from the distant past.

"We were taking bets on when this could have been made, sir," one crewman draped in a brown cloth pipes up, "I think it's from the Glass Wars."

"Fuck off, it's far too old for that, I'd say twenty-ninth century...at least," another butts in with a deep baritone voice.

"What about you Keller?" I ask the Engineer sitting himself down. Keller puts a gloved hand to his face, rubbing more grease onto it.

"I'd say...Reclamation," he guesses, putting his hand to his chin in a comedic fashion. The group howls in laughter at the idea.

"Reclamation! Fuck you! Something like that doesn't survive that long out there!" the man to my right yells.

For the last time, the call to arms is sounded!
For the fight, we all stand prepared!

"I like that idea," I say, and the laughter dies down, eyebrows raise. "I'd say it's Reclamation too."

"Well, looks like you win, Keller," another jokes. "Captain has final say. Reclamation it is. We're listening to the original Aryans."

"There's no way to know for sure," I state, not wanting the festivities to end just yet. "So, what are we betting?" I ask. "Just so I know what we get if we win." I point to Keller and me.

"The finest German whiskey, aged twelve years, winner gets the bottle," Keller states, holding up a fine brown bottle with the engraving of an eagle. An idea pops into my head. There is a way that we could figure out this little mystery...or at least, the best-educated way to.

"I have a way to settle this," I say. "My brother Ulric. Knights have all that knowledge of Reich history over any of us buffoons. He might help." Drunken agreement arises from the crowd.

"I'll go wake him up!" the man to my right eagerly says, but before he stands I place a hand on his shoulder.

"If some random sailor he doesn't know knocks on his door at this time of night, I guarantee he won't come out, and we'll never learn the secret," I joke. "I'll do it."

With that, I lift myself up, excuse myself from the group who raise their drinks to me, and turn back toward the portway into the officer quarters.

The joyous song still plays behind me. It must have been some crazy bastard, to go out into the desert to get that. Yes, it was "illegal" to take objects from the sand, but nobody really bothered to scavenge anyway. Going out without a ship oftentimes was just suicide.

A decent suit of armor was really the best and only defense against the scalding heat outside, and at best it lasted a few hours. After that, the last bit of power runs out, the cooling systems fail, and the suit's occupant succumbs to the heat in a matter of minutes.

Who would want to risk their own life to try to find something out there? Everything interesting, like old ships and lost civilizations once under the sea, had supposedly been picked clean long ago. Who would expect that after two thousand years, there would still be objects out there left undiscovered? Something potentially from the Reclamation—from the time of the Eternal Führer and the founding of the Reich? The time when Europeans reclaimed their land from the influence of foreign outsiders....

It was a difficult time. Everything changed so rapidly. Technology, culture, society as a whole. Records from that time were simply lost over the thousands of years. Now only the legends, the book *My Struggle*, and the dams remained as a testament to that time we can only imagine now.

The origins of the Aryans have always been wrapped in a bit of mystery because of that. So to have something from that time, to hear those voices speaking back to us...if it was actually true... that'd be a remarkable find.

I stroll down to the special chambers where the officers sleep and find myself in a dimly lit, empty hallway. Most of the occupants are out on the deck or stuck in the Bridge. I really should get back to Volker and Witzel, yet my curiosity is getting the best of me.

I reach a metal door and knock softly on it with three rhythmic hits. There is no response. After a minute of waiting, the door slowly opens, revealing a puzzled Ulric. He has disbanded his armor for the night. His eyes, half shut, look back at me as he scratches at his disheveled hair. Looking past him, I see inside his quarters a book placed upon his mattress. It looks like a copy of *My Struggle*.

"What is it?" he asks, resting an exhausted hand on his forehead. "I was about to sleep."

"Not socializing with the crew, huh?" I say with a smile to a sleepy Ulric. He looks back at me, unresponsive. Mouth agape.

"Not particularly," he yawns after a few seconds. "I was just reading, it's pretty late."

"It's only 22:00," I chuckle. "Nobody sleeps this early."

"Two hours to read before bed. I was on the section where the Führer discusses how peace in Europe came to be."

"Want to use that reading for some good?" I say. Ulric's eyebrows perk up, and he straightens himself up just a little bit.

"What do you mean?" he asks, an inflection of curiosity coming through his tired voice.

"First Engineer Keller somehow got in the possession of this old black disc," I explain, putting my hands in the shape of the circular object. "It plays a song, and nobody can place when it was made."

"And this can't wait 'til tomorrow because..."

"A twelve-year-old whiskey is on the line," I flat out admit.

Ulric stares at me blankly, blinks a few times slowly, and begins to close the door. My hand goes to catch it.

"The song might be from the Reclamation," I quickly explain, just before the metal hatch shuts. A gap still persists, before Ulric swings open the door again, snapping himself out of his stupor. He looks at me with wide eyes at the sound of the word.

"You're joking?" he asks, his tone shifting to excitement.

"Not at all, that's why we need you. You're the scholar here," I say.

Ulric stands frozen. I can tell the cogs must be turning. He looks to his bed, and then back to me.

"Damn it," he curses under his breath. "Wait here." And with that he shuts the door.

Back on the deck, I lead Ulric past the other fires and toward the group with the booming song. They notice we've arrived and raise their drinks yet again, welcoming Ulric in. He nods to the men. I can tell his main focus is on whatever the artifact must be, as he sits down on a stool. I join him.

"My brother caught the best of my curiosity. Damn him," Ulric says. "So what am I looking at?"

"That is an audio device," Keller answers in a satisfactory tone, pointing with pride at the unremarkable combination of wood, wire, and a horn fitted on top. "I made it myself, took a couple months." The song continues on with its melody:

> *Raise the flag! The ranks tightly closed!*
> *The SA march with quiet, steady step.*
> *Comrades shot by the Red Front and reactionaries*
> *March in spirit within our ranks.*
> *Clear the streets for the brown battalions,*
> *Clear the streets for the storm division!*
> *Millions are looking upon the swastika full of hope,*
> *The day of freedom and of bread dawns!*
> *For the last time, the call to arms is sounded!*
> *For the fight, we all stand prepared!*
> *Already Hitler's banners fly over all streets.*
> *The time of bondage will last but a little while now!*

Ulric sits as stiff as a flagpole, focused in concentration. It was a posture I was all too familiar with when we were children. Every situation, any question was met with a posture that could only mean he was focusing all his energy to reach the answer. As the song came to an end and we were met with silence, Ulric remained with his face in his hands.

"I'm trying to think back to my time scouring the Reich records," Ulric remarks, baffled and confused. "All the chants and songs, the speeches from past Führers, and...yet..."

"Yet what?" I insist, awaiting the answer. The rest of the group leans in just a tad closer toward my brother.

"Yet I'm blanking!" he insists, his eyebrows raised at the prospect. "I'm not familiar with this, or quality of the audio. Everything I've ever heard had such clear audio that it could have taken place right in front of me, even songs from thousands of years ago. Unless..."

"Unless...this was recorded before the official records," the freckled man says in a slurred voice.

"You all think this was recorded during the Reclamation?" Ulric asks.

"I still think it's Glass Wars," another chimes in.

"Well, Keller and I do," I say, lending a hand to the grease-faced, missing-toothed grinning man across the fire. "So, what do you think, S.S. Knight?" I ask Ulric.

The group leans in a little bit more with bated breath, waiting to hear the verdict.

"They do mention something about 'clearing the streets,' and such a song wouldn't make sense if all the Reich's enemies were already outside our borders."

"But," a man with a crooked nose interrupts, "it also said 'the call to arms,' so a battle. Glass Wars."

"You idiot, that could mean Reclamation too," Keller debates, pointing his empty pint across the fire.

"I mean, the Reclamation was largely a peaceful affair," Ulric teaches. "It was just the expulsion of the Scavengers and uniting the countries under the Reich. The Eternal Führer never mentioned anything about violence in his book."

He begins flipping through his copy of *My Struggle*.

"There are a few passages in the Eternal Führer's words that could be construed as violent. I theorize, however, that it's mostly just about the defense of the country against foreigners, not outright violence. Like a metaphorical war, not a literal one, since he did unite Europe in the end through peace," Ulric lectures to nobody in particular, perhaps just rationalizing a conclusion to himself.

"Damn," Keller says with a tone of defeat, "guess it is the Glass Wars." He prepares to hand the whiskey bottle to the freckled man.

"Well...hang on...," Ulric interrupts, pointing up a finger, "this audio is far too muffled. Where did you find it?"

"I didn't find it, it was sold to me," Keller replies.

"Where did they find it?" Ulric asks.

"In the desert."

Ulric's eyes widen, and he leans forward with hands covering the lower half of his face. Letting out a groan, he runs his hands through his hair as he looks back to me.

"You know this is illegal, right?" he says to me with a disappointed expression, his face falling flat.

"I know," I reply, not bothering to come up with an excuse.

"We aren't supposed to take anything from the desert. You know that you're putting me in a very difficult situation," he lectures.

"It's fine, Ulric," I insist, attempting to downplay the entire thing. It wasn't that big of a deal. I knew that Ulric would have a fit over the law being broken; however, I wanted to know when this disc was created...and also...you know...whiskey. He looks at me strangely, but composes himself and turns back to the group.

"Can I see the disc at least?" Ulric asks, his mannerisms laced with begrudging annoyance.

"Of course!" Keller accepts, opening up the hatch on the box yet again. He reaches inside and pulls out the black disc with a small hole in the center. Keller bends over the fire and places the disc in Ulric's hands. Ulric examines it as if he was scanning over a book, feeling the circular ridge lines and touching its glossy, smooth surface.

"It's not damaged. So that's good," he concludes, his eyes squinting at the artifact.

"What are you looking for?" one of the men asks impatiently. "I want my whiskey."

"I'm trying to see what could cause the muffled audio," Ulric defends. "I mean, if this really was during the Glass Wars, we'd have clear audio. Oldest audio I heard was from the twenty-second century...I think...and that was perfect quality. This, however...this sounds so distant. Maybe it was your box that caus—"

"Nah ah ah," Keller insists, cutting off Ulric. "This thing was hand-crafted by me. It works perfectly. Don't question my craftsmanship."

"I can't prove otherwise...but if that's the case then, simply based on the poor audio...this might very well be from the Reclamation," Ulric concludes, handing the disc back to a celebratory Keller. He and I both cheer, at the expense of the others' protests.

"Oh come on, of course he's going to say that because he's your brother!" one of them says.

"I assure you, Ulric cares very little about the whiskey. Now if you please," I say, reaching my hand out for the bottle. "I'm going to share this with everyone." This seems to calm the entire group.

"Good save, Captain." Keller jokes, handing me the bottle.

Rounds are given and shots are taken around the fire. The song continues to play on repeat as men joke about. Ulric, however, sits next to me, drink still full in hand, eyes locked onto the small brown box.

"Still trying to figure it out?" I lean over to ask him.

"No, I'm trying to analyze what I should do. That is illegal contraband," he whispers.

"You don't need to do anything, this is my ship. I don't need to deal with any stress from laws."

"This is still Reich property—you'll just disobey a law? I thought you were devoted to the Reich?"

"More devoted to the moral laws, not the literal laws."

"So you just pick and choose?"

"That's the best you can do out here. Don't you think what a waste in history it is that we can't just take stuff from the desert anyway?"

"Of course, but it's not my job to question the law."

"It's not your job to enforce it either. You're just a scholar, and a Knight."

"Knights can enforce it out of principle."

"Well, can you leave the principal alone for a bit, at least until we get back to shore? I don't want to deal with you making enemies by smashing the disc."

"I guess. It is a tremendous find...if it really was from that time... I'm at a loss for words if it was," Ulric admits, his face changing into a smile at the thought. I think the idea of the illegality of it is taking a back seat to the prospect this might be historical. "I've spent so much of my life reading over the words of the Eternal Führer...imagine these men knew him."

"That'd truly be a find," I admit, taking out a cigar from my pocket.

"Imagine what Hitler must have been like to the people back then," Ulric wonders, looking down at his copy of *My Struggle*, seeing the painted image of Adolf Hitler. Hitler's blond hair was combed neatly as he stood against a red and gold flag.

"One of the first original Aryans," he continues on, losing himself in his thoughts. "That song..."

"That song is one of a kind," I say, lighting my cigar. Ulric looks down at the book. He goes quiet.

"Why was that song forgotten?" Ulric mutters, trailing off. "How is it that something like that can just disappear from the records?"

"Anything can be forgotten, Ulric," I say, handing him a shot of whiskey. He takes it with one hand, holding his book in the other.

"I guess so," he accepts, before downing the drink. The glasses clank over the small makeshift fire. The flames release bits of ash and smoke off into the painted night sky.

Whispers from the Past

The canyon is only a few days away, and already it is making its presence known. As we travel further south, the endless flat plains of salt and sand begin to crack into a series of shallow ravines. They carve up the ground like the occasional piece of flesh cut from a body. Twisting natural bridges soon will become the only route that this ship can take, but for now the terrain is flat. Eventually the options we have will become more limited.

The key to a good captain is knowing how to navigate the ship when those paths become narrow. Which ground is the safest to take? How far are we from the gully down below? One wrong error and the ship could find itself on a treacherous perch or an unstable cliffside. Another mistake and many have found themselves tumbling down into the gully below.

Sometimes the safest and only path is to simply hug the cliffs of the peninsula before eventually reaching the smooth hills into the canyon.

The Descent awaits us. A canyon so vast and wide that in some areas, the cliffs are gradual enough to be traveled by ships. It's a path on a smooth slope that takes us right into the belly of the canyon, and the deepest place on land. Yet for now, the only cliffs I see are the mile-high rocky walls, the remnants of coastline from the old Italen peninsula.

I stand near the bow, peering up into a clear summer day. The air is so clear, and I think I can make out the remains of villages that once lined the beach which now adorns the top of the cliffs like whispers from the past. Husks of old villas and houses, they are all are engulfed in the sand.

"Are you going to just stand out there in your power armor, sir?" Volker's rasping voice cracks through the radio in my helmet.

"Wanted some fresh air, First Officer, stretch my legs for a bit," I respond in a monotone fashion.

"That's some quality air you're getting inside that helmet," he jokes.

"We make do with the cards we're handed," I respond.

I appreciate my helmet. This desert reflects the scorching sun so much that I doubt whether, without this layer of glass between my eyes, I would even be able to see. To view the bowsprit that juts out like a sword toward whatever lies ahead. To see the red-and-gold flags fluttering from it in the wind. I inspect the large cannons, artillery, and anti-aircraft guns scattered across the front.

My footsteps take me toward the starboard side of the ship. From this angle, I can simply look down and watch the revolutions of the treads. Their thick metallic hide pushing us forward with every turn. Sand beneath crunching and swirling as it is tossed into the air. A cloud continuously rising from where the machine greets the ground—it travels at least a mile into the air, like a volcano erupting in the ocean.

I walk back inside the Bridge, taking off my helmet to hear the full extent of the wind coming inside. Volker is sitting casually in a small chair near the dashboard. Ulric is sitting by the door to the stairway, his head deep in a book. His hand is propped against the side of his temple, as if he is about to fall asleep. Trips usually are long and tedious affairs.

"You should get a view of the towers on the horizon, port side," Volker remarks, casually pointing toward me.

"Towers?" I ask in confusion. The word seems to have awoken the sleepy Ulric as well, who perks up from his slumber.

"Eagle Nest #9," Volker simply states, looking at me, then toward something in the distance behind me. I turn backward toward where he is pointing. Sure enough, there is a blurry series of figures on the horizon. They rise up like trees on a field of white. Were they not destroyed years ago, those dark towers might be rising even higher.

Ulric stands next to me, his hands pressed against the glass to get a good enough view of those black objects rippling against the desert heat.

"I've never seen an Eagle Nest before," he says, excited.

"That's not a very good first impression," I remark, looking off toward the half-standing buildings.

"I don't care, they still look magnificent," Ulric admits, his face contorted into an excited smile. I stare off at them with a pain in my stomach.

"Should have seen them when they were actually standing," Volker says behind us.

The first time I saw an Eagle Nest I was storming one with a rifle in my hand. The giant stone statues towered over me as I scaled those massive steps. The fighting was intense in the central tower. It was like fighting in the middle of a city square. Nests are practically just cities.

Remnants of a time when the Reich tried to colonize the desert, perhaps terraform the Kiln into a suitable grassy plain. In reality, they simply became islands in a new ocean of sand. Yet, where most people would be dismayed by the hardships, Aryans accept the challenge.

Their giant stone towers house everything that a resident would need. Schools, hospitals, apartments, military garrisons. They know the danger that living out here can pose, but they don't seem to mind. In fact, they seem to revel in the chance to defend the Reich against invaders.

They're descendants of pioneers after all—it makes sense. Fervent believers in spreading the culture of the Reich. In a way, the collection of Nests that line the entire southern border of the Reich has become a defensive perimeter. The Nests do their best to keep out any unwanted Scavenger ships from crossing into the Kiln. Yet, some always do slip through.

We all look on at Eagle Nest #9, its crumbling towers a symbol of one of the few times the colonists couldn't hold back a foreign attack.

"I don't know why they don't simply rebuild it," Volker complains, spinning around in his chair.

"Maybe because it's a reminder of what the Scavengers can do," Ulric theorizes.

"Yeah, sure is a good reminder, when nobody can see it except the ships who need a supply refill. Now ships just have to wait until the Nests on the other side of the canyon."

"Sacrifices for remembrance, I suppose," Ulric guesses, taking his face off of the glass and placing himself back on his seat.

"I like practical gestures that don't force us to pack a week more of supplies," I remark, rubbing my eyes. I had a restless sleep last night. Tossing and turning on my cot. Slowly my feet carry me back to the dashboard, and to the seat at the very center, the Captain's chair, where I plop myself down.

"Well, I like the grand symbolic gestures," Ulric admits, placing the book back on his lap. "Reminds us what dangers lie out there for Aryans."

"True, and I'm going to hate myself if I don't get off of this Bridge. Let me go stretch my legs to symbolize my watch being over," Volker says, putting on his helmet. My stomach growls and I realize I haven't eaten a single thing today.

"If you're going down to the cafeteria, get me something," I ask Volker, to which he gives an agreeable "alright" and disappears as the door closes behind him. I'm left alone with the hum of the ship's engine and my brother. We don't say much to one another. My attention is focused on the winding hills of dunes up ahead.

"So," Ulric says to me, cutting through the silence.

I turn to him, my expression a mix of boredom and lack of sleep. I respond with a "Yes?"

"What do you do around here...to pass the time?" he asks, putting down his book and looking at me. I glance around, leaning over in my seat to grab a bottle of beer. I hold it out, shaking it in a signifying manner.

"Drink mostly," I say. "What you saw yesterday."

This answer doesn't seem to really quench Ulric's curiosity, and he picks himself off of the chair and strolls around the Bridge. His hands have an odd twitch when he is bored; they shake around nervously, as if they need to do something. It's something he's had as long as I can remember. On long summer days in Germania with nothing to do, I had to babysit him, and there would go his hands.

"Do you ever...I don't know... maybe...," he ponders.

"No," I cut him off. "This is the desert. There isn't much to do. If you're bored, I can't help you."

Ulric walks around the room, examining each and every detail. I wouldn't be surprised if he started counting the buttons just to pass the time. The buzzing of the engine continues on.

"You enjoy this?" he asks. The question takes me aback. I sit up a little bit higher in my chair, and have a good laugh.

"Yes," I reply. "It's more entertaining than being some bookkeeper up north. What do you do to pass the time?"

"Read mostly," Ulric says. "I've already read through *My Struggle* a few times on this trip."

"Sounds like you should have brought another book," I laugh, taking a drink from the beer.

"Yeah, I should have," he says. "I've mostly just been thinking about this place. Do you ever do that?"

"What about this place?" I ask dully, putting down the beer.

Ulric strolls to the other side of the ship and looks out at the rocky cliffs. The dunes make their way up the endless wall. Ulric needs to bend himself down to get even a decent look at the blurry edge of the peninsula's edge.

"You ever think about what it was like when the sea disappeared?" Ulric asks, still crouched and looking upward.

"Not really," I lie. I do think about it a lot, however with the hunger pangs and the sleepless night, I'm not in the mood to discuss the fate of the Kiln with an overeager Ulric. Now, I am interested in the history of the Reich. It's interesting. However, Ulric always takes things too far. If one allows him, he will bring the conversation down a rabbit hole of pointless little details. I'm sure it's fitting for a chat with fellow Knights...but not with me.

"Oh," Ulric responds, disappointed. "I just see those small buildings up there and think about the people that once lived in them. Wonder what it was like to see the sea dry up."

"I mean, I think it was a long process," I respond, uninterested.

"Yes, I know that, it just must have been strange," he continues, not noticing I'm paying more attention to the bottle than to his remarks. "I imagine a grandparent explaining to his children's children about a time when the sea was at their doorstep. Then those children's children had their own offspring and the cycle began anew. Centuries of villagers telling about how close the sea once was, until there was nothing left."

"They probably left long before the sea dried up entirely," I say. "Not much to think about."

"I mean, it was for a better purpose, for the Atlantropan dams, but still, it must have been hard for them. Sometimes you don't think about the sacrifice that was needed to make the world a better place."

"Well, I'm getting paid, so that's good," I joke, trying to end the conversation.

"You don't even care to think about this at all?" Ulric says, turning around.

I swivel my head toward him. "I do," I say. "It's just, you go overboard sometimes whenever there is a discussion about Reich history."

"You didn't think it was such a bad thing yesterday," Ulric snaps back, his eyes narrowing.

"Yeah...well..." I try to think of a way to excuse that. "It was for an important reason."

"You just wanted to win the whiskey, didn't you," Ulric accuses. To this, I laugh.

"No!" I chuckle. "That disc could have been from the Reclamation. Just because a bottle happened to be on the line, doesn't mean anything."

"Right," Ulric replies, not believing me. "As an Aryan it's important to be passionate about our culture. Not just about alcohol and prostitutes."

"Where is this coming from?" I remark, laughing at the absurdity of that sentence.

"I mean, you aren't the most lawful Aryan...now, are you?" Ulric accuses.

My eyes squint down at him as I lift myself out my chair. "What is that supposed to mean?" I growl, my armor-clad body barreling toward him. His frame was smaller and weaker than my own—if I really wanted to, I could snap him like a twig, just like that whore. Yet Ulric stands his ground, fists clenched and head held high. I stop just before I get within breathing distance of him.

He knows that. He knows that I can't touch him. Because he is family.

"I mean...," he says, attempting to find the most diplomatic way of telling me off. "You don't seem to care about the actual laws of the Reich. You are fine with having an illegal artifact on your ship. You disrespect Aryan women, even if they are...misguided in their professions.... You drink and smoke even though that would never be acceptable up in Germania...."

I lean in close to his skinny face, looking him deep in his small, blue eyes. "I do enough for the Reich," I hiss. "I served in the military. I captain this ship. I fight Scavengers and make our enemies suffer. That is enough."

"Do you do that for the Reich or yourself? When was the last time you read *My Struggle*? Can you even name a philosophy or quote of Adolf Hitler?" Ulric lectures, pointing to the book near the door. The engine continues to hum throughout the cabin.

My eyes, unflinching, lock onto his. I can feel my heart beating hard in my chest, like it wants to leap out and strangle him. If this were anybody but my own brother, I would have thrown him through the glass. Yet he knows that. He knows that I can't touch him. Because he is family.

"Hitler talked about defending the tribe against the foreign hordes. That's what I do," I mutter, wiping my forehead clear of the sweat dripping down.

"He talked about respecting the tribe as well. Hitler wanted peace among Europeans. That's why he built the dams. He didn't build Atlantropa so it could become your escape from the Reich," Ulric says. His tone is becoming one of a typical Knight, lecturing as if they are keepers of the entire world. Masters of knowledge. It annoys me to no end.

"I don't need the rest of the Reich," I spit. "The Kiln is where I thrive. If you don't like it, you don't need to come back. But until then, you're stuck with me. Under my leadership."

"Well, while I'm here, you should read the book. You might learn something about being a decent Aryan." And with that, Ulric walks past my hunched-over figure, puts on his helmet that was placed next to the book, and walks off of the Bridge, leaving me alone with my thoughts and that hum.

The Orange Fog

As the sun rippled over the horizon, we too crested over the final slope of the Descent. We had spent days cramped up in the ship, unable to leave. It appeared like a fine, flat plain. But it was deceiving. The temperature was so high that even going outside with a suit would spell the end of an unlucky sailor. All that matters now is that we made it out.

The gradual incline levels off into an expanse of flat, sandy desert. Unlike the land up north, where cliffs form a wall around the white landscape, this region of the Kiln has far less...anything. We're in the southern portion now. The area closest to the continent of Africa. There are no cliffs, there are no landmarks of any kind—our instruments and a dust storm far in the distance are our only aids in navigation. Without them, we wouldn't even know what direction we were going in.

I stand on the Bridge, arms to my side, joined by the usual ensemble of Volker, Witzel, and Ulric. I examine a pristine, barren world devoid of any imperfection. Just one canyon could ruin its purity, one crack in this uniform plain—but no. It is as flat as a marble tabletop, and just as smooth.

There is almost a pang of guilt in my stomach at the thought of tearing a trail through such an untouched landscape with the ship's mechanical treads. Volker and Witzel stare at the storm ahead. Ulric looks out the window. We have rarely talked since our fight a few days ago. Not an ideal Aryan in the mind of my own brother? What a joke. I don't need to abide by his views of peace and prosperity like those Knights up north do. Could I read Hitler's book more often? Of course. But I seem to neglect doing that, when I have the job of commanding this ship. It's easy for a kid to lecture me on failing at my duties as an Aryan when all he needs to worry about is studying that book.

For now, I have other troubles. For example, the sandstorm is slowly migrating closer, swirling around like a beast, making its way across the untouched salt and sand. It's a wall of orange, as tall as the dams of Maria. I can hear the winds howl outside the

Bridge's metal walls. Flags frantically dance as they are caught up by the gusty anticipation.

Storms are no issue for the ship. It is just sand and wind, enough for the *Howling Dark* to handle. We have already been through five or so on this journey alone. Yet they are still an inconvenience. Visibility drops to zero. I always prefer for us to get out of the storm quickly, and for that we'll need to hug the edge.

"We should turn a bit to the left," I command, staring out the window. "Hug the edge of the storm and try to avoid as much of it as possible."

Volker, standing at the wheel of the ship, nods in understanding and adjusts course. The ship slowly begins to veer to the left, turning to reach the edges of the incoming storm. The wall is large, and right in front of us. There is no possibility that we can avoid it. It's much too wide for that. But if it is going to hit us, we might as well make the best of it.

It is still a few kilometers away.

As it comes closer, the desert floor ripples from the new gusts of wind. They blow toward our ship and cascade over the deck. I can see the edges of the storm, but it is too distant for us to reach it in time. It's moving too fast toward us, and we're too far away to escape.

After a half hour or so, the entire storm fills our horizon. It looms over us all like a behemoth about to swallow us up. The morning sun has disappeared over the clouds and we are enwrapped in a long, dark shadow from the storm. It's as if we are in a valley in front of a mountain, and the *Howling Dark* continues on. We can't turn back to avoid it—that would only drive us back into the Descent. The best course of action is to barrel through as fast as this ship's treads can carry us. The Reich flag flutters at the ship's bowsprit, the golden swastika glinting against the last rays of sunlight we have left.

The storm arrives. The cliffside of churning sand falls down upon us like a rolling wave. The wind hits with tremendous force, sending anything not tied down on the deck tumbling about. Metal walls screech like an animal wishing nothing more than to devour.

Visibility drops as the thick orange fog envelopes the ship, and yet we continue on. This area is flat for miles, so it's unlikely we'd accidentally roll into an unknown canyon or hole. All we need to do is keep up speed and make it past this, blinded or not.

A few minutes pass. The Bridge is silent.

"What is that?" Volker softly mutters, pointing off into the storm.

"What is what?" I ask, whirling around and pacing right next to him. My eyes scan the area where his fingers are pointing .

"I thought I saw something," he remarks, quietly. "Like there was a light through that sandstorm."

Through the fog, clouded by swirling currents of sand, a shrouded, dark, muffled object is slowly moving in the opposite direction of our ship. It's only about a kilometer away. The blurry mass is smaller than our ship, but far too large to be an animal...as if animals could survive out here.

It's a vessel.

"Fuck," I curse. "It's a ship. Were there supposed to be any of our ships on this route?"

Volker flips through the travel logs for the Kiln, and puts his hand to his face in confusion.

"The route for any Reich ships going south is at least fifty kilometers away...there's no possibility that is one of our own... unless they got lost...which would sure be difficult to fuck up."

"Let me just check, so we're certain. We're in radio distance of Eagle Nest #13 right?" I ask him.

"I believe so," Witzel answers instead.

"Alright, I'll check. Get the men mobilized, however, if this is worst case scenario," I mutter to Volker, while still looking at the distant, blurry ship drifting across the desert floor.

I pick up the microphone on the radio. There might be a chance this is just a ship that got lost, but the feeling in my stomach as I look on is telling me differently.

"*Howling Dark* to Eagle Nest #13," I mutter into the radio. I wait for a response, as the white noise fizzles out of the speakers.

"Good morning, *Howling Dark*—this is Eagle Nest #13," a female voice coos through.

"I wanted to know if any ship routes had updated in the last few days," I respond, looking out the window. "We've spotted a ship about a kilometer east of us. Are there any ships scheduled in our location?"

There is more white noise and some soft talking for a few seconds, as if the woman is speaking to others about the routes.

"There are no ships scheduled to go south near your location at this time, *Howling Dark*. Closest one is *Taurus*, and that is a hundred kilometers southwest of you already into the Descent," the lady responds in a disappointed voice.

"That's what I was worried about," I say. "Put out a warning for this area, we certainly have a raider ship in the area."

"Right away, *Howling Dark*—we are dispatching warnings to all incoming ships. Stay safe. Sieg Heil," she ends.

"Sieg Heil," I finish, putting down the radio and looking off at the ever-growing cloud. So it is official: that ship is not one of ours.

Volker calls in a full mobilization of the crew. The air outside is so thick with sand that even the men running to their battle stations are obscured in the windy storm. It blows past the rising artillery and large metal cannons now raised toward the mysterious stranger at starboard.

Just as I look up from the deck, I see that the object has gotten thinner. They've turned. The savages have turned right toward us.

"The Scavengers must have snuck past the Eagle Nests using the storm." Volker announces in frustration.

"They can do that?" Ulric asks in bewilderment.

"The Nests aren't that close together," I respond. "They're mostly to attract raids, like flies to honey...it's not a wall. I don't know why they're coming this far north though."

"There's just sand here. Closest thing is #13, and that's what, fifty kilometers to the south?"

"Unless it's not trying to raid an Eagle Nest," I respond, my voice layered in irritation at the situation. "It could be hunting for ships."

"Should I call in an Aegir Drop?" a nervous Ulric asks me.

I shake off the suggestion. "No," I say, collecting myself, "We can take them ourselves."

"But—"

"I...said...no."

Ulric gives me a look of disapproval and walks away. I'm too distracted by the circumstances at hand to care about his concerns. This is a large ship—we can handle this ourselves as we always have. It may not be ideal fighting them in a storm, but it's not an impossible feat. As well, the *Howling Dark* hasn't been in a good fight in a while, and I'm itching for one.

The dark mass grows larger as it comes closer to our position. They most certainly are moving in for an attack.

"Alright," I announce calmly. "Witzel, get some main cannon fire on that dot."

"Time to send them a greeting," Volker jokes, followed by a mutter into the radio and a small, crackling voice squeaking in confirmation. I see, through the warm mist of the sand, the main cannons in the front deck rise from their horizontal position.

"Their location has been targeted. Primed and positioned to fire, Captain," Volker speaks to me.

"Fire," I mutter into the radio.

The void erupts into an explosion of bright yellows and white-hot flashes. Two thunderous pillars of fire and smoke erupt from the main cannons. The light from the flames reflect off the thick currents swimming around the men down below. Thick fog churning in an ocean of tiny, dusty particles, all of which ripple out from the shockwave produced by the guns.

All stumble, as the floor jolts by the cannon shots. It is a deafening roar that rattles our ship to its core. There is another pause. A few seconds waiting to see any blurry light in the distance, waiting to hear some sound.

Seconds go by. I feel every moment in the beating of my heart. Flicking lights begin to dance among the thick cloud. It is like a phantom slowly revealing itself. They have been hit.

Three bright flashes bloom from the soft flames, covered by a kilometer of sand. My stomach plunges like a rock into a deep creek. How did those shots not destroy them? They have always been able to take out Scavenger ships in a single barrage.

More seconds...my stomach drops even lower. It's as if lead has been planted directly into me.

Light sparkles out in three quick successions from the encroaching ship. More seconds. Bright flashes erupt around us. Shadows of the scrambling men appear, made solid for a brief moment as the explosions illuminate the ship in every direction. The roar of the blasts knocks all in the cabin off of our feet. Ulric flops onto the floor. I catch myself on a bar, holding myself up.

Pillars of flame shoot around the side of the deck. More seconds. I spring myself up to regain my balance and lunge toward the front window to examine the lower deck. Picking up the radio, I call for a status report—all respond that they are stable. We haven't been hit. The barrage missed. Now it's our turn.

"Prepare another barrage!" I order. Volker, already standing near the radio, cries out into the microphone.

More explosions from our guns. The ship veers sharply as we turn. All of us on the Bridge struggle to hold our feet. This barrage has to be the one—it has to be the one to knock them out.

More waiting. Bright flickers off in the distance. It appears too far for it to be a hit, though. Dammit.

"We need to pick up speed!" I call to Volker, who immediately pulls up the lever on the dash. The ship's treads spin even faster in an attempt to dodge whatever oncoming barrages are next.

The enemy ship is now only half a kilometer away and is closing in fast.

Lights in the distance, we swerve seconds later. One explosion is so bright against the darkness I need to cover my eyes. Another is so thunderous I lose my grip on the dashboard and go tumbling down. The final one I hear brightens the entire Bridge with a warm glow, followed by the sound of screeching metal. Fuck.

I bring myself to my knees, and the alarms blare into my eardrums. The radio chatter awakens as voices yell in muffled tones. We've been hit, but where? I order another barrage and keep my eyes on the ship, but I need to see the damage. I have a sinking feeling that I know where it is.

My helmet gets placed on my head and I open the door leading out of the Bridge, running across the balcony to get a view of the stern, only to be met with a small inferno. The stern's dock has been hit. Fuck.

The damage doesn't appear to be massive, but we've taken a direct hit. Flames rise from the shattered metal beams jutting out from the deck. Armored figures scatter about to douse the flames. Fucking Scavengers. Thank the Reich that this ship is large enough to sustain such blows.

As I stumble back to the Bridge, another round of our fire knocks me around, but I'm able to make my way back in...just in time to see tiny explosions connect with the incoming vessel.

"Fire again!" I yell, but before we can respond another time, there is a lull in the fire. The Scavenger ship hasn't retaliated. Through the warm mist, the orange glow from the incoming vessel appears to be growing. Within seconds, it becomes so bright it shines past the cloudy sand and becomes a white, shining light. The light fills up the Bridge as it shoots higher and higher above us all, mushrooming out as it grows. Then, as soon as it arrived, it disappears.

A deep boom radiates throughout the ship. The sand from the storm dissipates for a moment as the shockwave blasts it away. For a moment, I gaze upon the smoldering Scavenger ship still moving purely on momentum toward us. It was like a bowl of fire, the entire top deck utterly obliterated by our guns.

As the bulbous cloud grows, the treads beneath it give out and the ship flips onto its port side. The sand engulfs us once again, but the ship is so close we can make out bodies toppling off as the machine crumbles onto the ground. Some of them scatter about, running from the mountain of debris falling above them. A couple escape; many do not, as the steel slams onto them. Metal and steel screech like a wounded cat as the vessel crumples, concave, into itself. With a loud crash, the black mass lies still, leaning on its side as smoke rises from its broken husk.

The Scavenger ships are far different than our own. They appear more cobbled together. Unlike the Reich's, which have a basis in the ancient warships, the Scavenger ships are more jaded, with tall metal towers and spindly columns. This one is so close, I can even make out the numerous thin flags flying from it, although now they are engulfed in flames.

The deck down below breaks out into cheers as they witness the sight. We got them. Celebrations go around the Bridge as we congratulate one another on a good kill. The *Howling Dark* continues on its way past the wreckage of the enemy ship, leaving the Scavengers that survived to boil in the desert. What luck, as well. The sun was beginning to shine through the fog of the now-passing storm. Shadowed bodies run in panic around their destroyed machine. They won't have long to escape the Kiln's blistering heat, so I order that we send a rescue team to help the poor savages out.

"Alright, men," I announce through the radio. "Let's go get them."

Special Guests

The reconnaissance vehicle barrels away from the *Howling Dark*, leaving a cloud of dust in its wake. The six-wheeled, heavily armored truck is a necessary requirement for any ship out here. For example, let's say the ship is going down. No man wants to be stranded in the desert, of course. Without recharging, the cooling systems in the armor will shut off in thirty-two hours, leaving the unfortunate soul inside left to wither in the heat. When all else fucks up, that vehicle is the beast that lugs us all back north. That's why most men have simply nicknamed it "The Camel."

I stand at the bow, observing in the distance a thin wisp of smoke floating like a snuffed-out candle. We should reach the crash site in a matter of minutes, but the storm is dispersing and I don't want to lose any guests.

Who is to say one of them won't succumb to their injuries by then? I can't allow them to escape their fate that easily. The fuming crew around me appears to agree.

Many pleaded to me for the opportunity of capturing the survivors; it was quite difficult picking just seven from an ecstatic bunch. Those that remain onboard crowd around me on the bow, eagerly awaiting the arrival of our special guests. Everyone wishes to get the first glimpse of The Camel coming back to the ship. They stare at the crash site like hyenas surrounding a corpse, laughing and chittering in anticipation.

I grasp my hands behind my back and contemplate how exactly these Scavengers could be punished. A sanding is the simple way, but I have already done so many sandings. Alright, one will be sanded, but the rest I want to experiment with. We have a few more days before the Descent anyway—might as well have some fun. I examine my metallic arm, imagining it being driven into the eye sockets of one of them. Such an image of them grasping at their bloodied face fills me with a primal, carnal flame of ecstasy.

Chants for retribution from my crew fill the air, thick as the dust churned up by the treads. They are rightfully furious, because they were almost obliterated by a cowardly attack. I've never seen a ship come this far to hunt for cargo. Sometimes farther south they will try to pick off lone ships, but never those coming right out of the Descent.

"Have you heard anything yet, sir?" one of the men, a grizzled veteran with a rusting brown arm, asks me. Others cheer at this question. They are awaiting the confirmation from The Camel that they have found survivors.

"Not yet," I declare.

I can hear the buzzing of chatter inside of my helmet. The Camel is in direct communication with our radio channel. When they reach the crash site and find any survivors, we'll know.

"What are you going to do to them, Ansel?" the collected voice of Ulric asks me, cutting through an inferno of angry chants.

"I don't know yet," I respond, lost in a pool of my own imagination.

My brother's silvery figure glides next to me, joining in the observation.

"Does that mean you are unsure of what their punishment will be, or does that mean you are unsure of how you will kill them?"

"Is that not the same thing?" I ask, confounded by such a question.

"The first means you might kill them, and the second means you've already made up your mind."

"Why would I not kill them?" I chuckle at the absurdity of his rhetoric. "They tried to kill our crew, they tried to kill you."

"Now hear me out. I think this could be an interesting opportunity," Ulric theorizes, like an old scholar. "The Knights have always wanted to study on live subjects, but well, you all kill them."

"I don't like where you're going with this."

"I'm just saying, we would bring them back to Germania, in chains of course, and the Knights might like to study them."

"Study them?"

"I know Knights that could experiment with them in a controlled space. See what their IQs are, observe how they think, and then, after we are done, maybe dissect them and look at what is going on inside those Scavenger brains."

"Don't see the use there is in that," I spit, "They're savages, they're like flies, remember? How much is there to learn from them?"

"Science about the different races was largely lost after the Reclamation. We don't have much data on how much the Scavengers differ from Aryans, psychologically of course. Today, we barely have the chance to secure a live specimen to study. Sailors simply kill them before they head back to shore."

"Yeah, because letting a Scavenger back into the Reich is suicide and nobody wants that burden on their head," I suggest in a tone of annoyance. How can he be thinking of such a thing? There doesn't need to be much research on why Aryans and non-Aryans are different.

"They'd be in a military prison, of course," Ulric attempts to reassure me.

"Sounds like mercy to me," I mutter.

"I can assure you it isn't that," he pleads.

"We already have limited supplies and it is for our own men," I argue, maintaining my calm demeanor in the presence of the crew. "Let me see how many we pick up. We'll bring them aboard. I'll decide what happens to them."

"Just give me one. That's all I'm asking," Ulric pushes. "It will give me something to do on the ship at least."

"I'll think about it," I respond. It is a convincing argument, as much as I hate to admit. Having Ulric away from the Bridge for once would be a relief.

"Thank you, Ansel," he says, reassured. His violet cape ripples in the desert wind.

"After that sneak attack though," I continue on, "I doubt the crew will let him stay alive for long."

Before Ulric can say another word, the radio crackles inside my helmet and I put up a finger to signify that he should be quiet.

"*Howling Dark, this is Camel 1, we've reached the ship,*" a muffled voice announces through the static. "*We've spotted a few Scavengers clinging to the ship. Some are running away. We're in pursuit.*"

"Understood," I swiftly respond, not wishing to waste any time. "Proceed with caution Camel 1."

I attempt to tune out the wails and whoops from my men behind me. They are a jumbled collection of oxidized metal and tattered cloth. Under each and every helmet is a man anxious for revenge.

They laugh as they see the vehicle barrel toward the burning mess of steel and flames. Dark ants scatter away from The Camel as it punches its way through the crowd. The clang of armor, rifles, and boots resonates from the radio.

I assume this is the troops exiting the back of the Camel. There is an indecipherable exchange of commands, followed by silence. I tensely await a response.

"*The ship is intact,*" the voice murmurs in an effort to remain unheard. "*The outside vicinity is clear, we're moving up.*" More scuffling.

I notice little flashes coming from the ants. Suddenly, a wild howl bursts forth inside my helmet as the radio buzzes with the crackling of passing bullets. Screaming, then commands, then more shots. Gunfire.

"*One of them is firing from behind the ship! Return fire! Return fire!*"

The next half-minute is an orchestra of gunfire. Even without the radio, we can hear the echoes of this exchange, which catch the interest of the crew. The earlier jeering has now been replaced by rumbling confusion.

"What's happening, Captain?" another man asks.

"Quiet," I bark at him, dedicating my entire attention to the radio feed.

"*He's down,*" another voice confirms.

"Was anyone hit?" I ask.

"*No, sir,*" the main voice responds. "*Enemy hip-fired at us, by luck only hit the ground around us. We're moving into the ship, the back of it is blown out.*"

"None of our men were hit, it was just one fucker who couldn't shoot for anything. He's down now," I announce to the awaiting crowd, which explodes into celebratory cheers.

I listen further, as the voices from the radio ascend sharply into a fury of blaring commands. They yell at something, and the something yells back.

"*HANDS UP. GET OUT OF THERE WITH YOUR HANDS UP.*" The command is repeated over and over by our men. I picture how terrified the battered and injured survivors must be inside that ship. Such an image makes me chuckle with satisfaction.

"*Five Scavengers are alive, sir. They tried running to the ship, but we got them. Most are battered and bruised but appear alright. They surrendered and we're loading them onto The Camel now. HANDS UP.*"

"Good work, Camel 1. Looking forward to the package delivery," I congratulate them, and then spin around to the crowd of twenty or so helmets, each glowing visor peering at me. All they need is the news. My arms are outstretched in a grandiose display, the metallic one glinting in the sun. I howl loud enough for all to hear.

"We're having guests over, men!" I shout. They cheer.

After The Camel arrives back, I order over the radio for the prisoners to be taken up to the deck. So that no Scavenger is unceremoniously bludgeoned by an enthusiastic sailor, I tell each and every man to stay calm when the captives arrive. If there is anything that can taint this day, it's the boring effectiveness of mob justice. This had to be a theatrical affair. Entertainment for all on such a long journey. For the rest of the day, this ship will be the Coliseum—we the lions.

"*Bringing them up now, sir,*" a voice confirms.

"Understood," I respond back.

The hatch in the central deck springs open, and the crowd becomes restless. I bellow for calm, and their voices die down. From the hatch comes the first one of our men, armed with a rifle and clad in his armor, a red cloth slung over his right shoulder. He barks down into the hole, pointing his rifle before proceeding forward. In his wake follows a group of five small, brown creatures, all chained together in a line. Each stumbles onto the deck.

The Scavengers' eyes are wide in shock. The whites of their eyes contrast like the full moon in a night sky against their charred complexions. I've never seen them so up close before. The man in the red cloth jabs the one in front and the line hobbles faster toward the bow of the ship, where I await them. Jeers and insults permeate from the crowd; however, by my orders, nobody else lays a hand on them.

"Remember that we can study them," Ulric says in a last effort.

"I told you we will see," I retort, my temper reaching a boiling simmer like this desert heat.

The line of hunched-over captives navigate through a parting in the crowd. Some hang their heads low toward the metal deck; others look around in confusion at the situation before them. All wear tattered and bloodied clothes. The red-cloaked man points his gun again and gestures for them to kneel. They understand that gesture and comply.

I raise one hand up and my men go silent. Only the rumbling of the treads and the whistling of the desert wind can be heard. I ponder what might be going through their minds at this moment. Are they terrified? Are they confused? Do they even understand existence like a human, or are they reacting more on instinct like frightened cats? Fuck, maybe Ulric had a bit of a point.

My mind wanders to how this situation might appear from their perspectives. Every man is covered in rusted armor. We tower over them all. The visors of our helmets are alight with the colors of red and blue. What a sight that would be to them.

They all are sweating profusely. Each armpit is soaked with perspiration. Being exposed to the Kiln's heat for so long must be an agonizing experience. We're in a basin, a cooker. The heat is incomparable to anywhere else. Not even wildlife can adapt to it. After a few minutes, the hallucinations will set in; after thirty minutes comes heatstroke; and after an hour follows certain death. However, these savages won't be lucky enough to live that long.

As I contemplate this, I hear through the silence a desperate, hushed voice and turn my head to the Scavenger farthest to the left. His head is pressed deep into his chained arms, and he is whispering a series of strange words. I can only make out a few... something about...a *yasue*...an *Ala*?

With a heavy stomp of my foot, I stroll slowly toward him. He is shaking, though he does not lift his head. What is he doing? I stand over him, his head just above my knee. I imagine stomping on him with one solid crunch, yet convince myself not to do it. Instead, I simply kneel down, reach out my metallic arm, and grab him by his coarse black scalp.

He lets out a cry and stares right into my dark helmet.

"HE...PRAYING!" a ragged voice desperately blurts out beside me...in broken German.

The sound cuts through the ship like a rock, and the crowd goes truly silent. A few gasp, and whispers spread like fire. I stay crouched down, confused at what I just heard. Did I just hear German words? I turn to face a grey-haired one, leaning forward with hands outstretched, staring right back at me.

"He is...*what*?" I angrily mutter, straightening up.

"He...praying. He... scared...," the greying Scavenger pleads. He has the pigment of bark from a tree. Years in the desert surely have done their work on the wrinkled skin and baggy eyes of this old man.

I turn to Ulric, confused. "How the hell is this Scavenger speaking German?" Before Ulric can respond, I bark to the old man. "How are you speaking German?" I repeat to him. He recoils at the sound and holds a hand up to his face. Pathetic. What is this?

"I...study...from...books...," he croaks.

"Books? What do you mean books?" I ask, with the inflection of a python's hiss.

"Books...they...come...from...big...towers...."

Eagle Nests, he's talking about Eagle Nests. How the hell did he get books from Eagle Nests? Did he steal them? Did he kill women and children to get to them?

"He's a fucking thief, cut his head off!" a voice yells from the back of the crowd, which responds in agreement.

"Wait!" Ulric pipes up, quickly moving toward me.

"He stole books from an Eagle Nest, he might have killed our own," I conclude.

"Keep him alive, we could find out something," Ulric pesters in a hushed voice.

"What if this is a trick?" I retort.

"How is speaking our language a trick?" Ulric whispers, confused. "And even if it is, we can get information from him. Study him."

"How did you obtain the books?" Ulric asks the quivering Scavenger.

"How...books?" he mutters in puzzlement.

"How did you *get* the books?" Ulric simplifies himself, making a gesture of holding a book.

The man continues his nervous shaking, and his eyes dart from one helmeted face to another.

"Bought...from market...merchant said...book...for children in... big towers...."

"A German schoolbook for kids," Ulric says to me.

"Yeah I can connect the dots," I say. "So they steal our stuff and sell it to their own people, the thieves."

"We need to keep him alive, keep him captive."

"No, Ulric."

"You don't understand how much of a waste it would be. Imagine how much we could gain from knowing their twisted psyche. We could find out where they hid more of those trinkets. Keep him isolated and I'll talk to him."

"Are we killing them or not?!" another voice rattles out, and the men grow restless.

"Hold on, I'm fucking thinking about this one," I shout back, pointing an armored finger to the kneeling Scavenger.

"So, what do you say?" my brother asks me.

"I say you're an idiot. But I admit I'm a bit curious as well. This better not fucking backfire on me," I argue.

"Thanks," Ulric says. "Do with the rest as you want."

"I plan on it. Let me ask him one more question," I conclude, turning to the Scavenger.

"Why did you attack us?"

He looks at me with worried eyes and stutters, attempting to conjure up the words.

"We...we...attack...because...," he blubbers out, looking at the floor, crestfallen.

"Thank you for that confirmation," I say. "We'll take care of your friends and you can stay with us. Take him away."

I motion for the red-cloaked guard to separate him from the group. The old Scavenger looks around, confused and shocked. I think he caught on to what I was saying. He screams in a foreign, blistering tongue to the rest of his kin, who begin to wriggle around, attempting to escape. They cry out in panic and anger, staring at my helmeted crew with dagger eyes.

With a swift motion, my fist connects with the closest one, his jaw cracks, and his head spins sharply away. Blood and teeth ooze from his gaping mouth. The rest of the prisoners quiet down, their brows now narrowed in anger—most are still shaking.

The old man is dragged away by the guard, and Ulric follows. The crowd parts for them and closes once again, hiding all three from sight. I have four culprits left before me who must pay for their crime. They cannot speak German; they are of no use to me.

"What should I do with them, men?!" I call out toward the mob, which meets this cry with a barrage of colorful suggestions.

"Gouge their eyes out!" one suggests.

"They can't shoot a gun without arms," rallies another.

Not recognizing our language but comprehending the tone of the crowd, some of the culprits wriggle uncomfortably in their chains. One of them looks at me with a sullen face. He seems perhaps Witzel's age, but his young face is engulfed in a ragged curly beard. One of his eyes is swollen shut and even though his skin is dark, large parts of it are bruised. As I face him, his expression evolves into one of pure contempt, as he growls under his breath in a string of incomprehensible gibberish. The message is clear, however—he is cursing at me. I guess we'll start with him.

"Unchain this one," I say to another crewmember who came from The Camel. His orange cloak trails behind him, fluttering in the wind. He unlocks the handcuffs from the young Scavenger and, with a forceful lift, he pulls the savage up onto his feet. As this happens, his friends' heads swivel from side to side. Some attempt to spit on me, while others plead in words I can't understand.

I grab the small neck of the Scavenger and yank him toward me. He pitifully attempts to jab at my armor with his fist, but instead grabs onto it in pain after colliding with my chest.

My hand tightens.

"I know you cannot understand me." I speak in a plain, calm voice down to the pirates. "However, I still feel the need to tell you all why you are here today. You are thieves. Leeching off of the efforts of civilization, meagerly and cowardly scarfing down table scraps like dogs. You cannot survive on your own without us, so you cling to our borders. You pillage our people, rape our women and children, and slaughter our men. I've seen your barbarity."

When I was a young man in the military, I remember storming that Eagle Nest to retake it from an infestation of Scavenger raiders. By the time we arrived it was already far too late. Most of the Nest had been depopulated. These creatures murdered a healthy colony of innocent people. That sickness I felt observing the hundreds of mutilated remains surges back into my stomach. They showed no mercy toward those children, and I will show no mercy today.

"Men," I speak to the crowd, "we aren't just punishing these *things* for their attack on our ship. We're avenging the countless lost in the raids on our people. Look at these Scavengers, some are old, imagine how many times they've attacked women and children. They have gotten away with their crimes for far too long."

I face the Scavenger whose head is at my chest. He is struggling to get away, perhaps jump over the side of the ship to safety, or what he thinks is safety. I lower my voice to only speak to him. He glares angrily into my glowing visor.

"Crimes do not go unpunished."

And with that I take his hand, the one that struck me, and contort it slowly and methodically, like the turn of the treads. On instinct, the Scavenger's body moves with it, trying with all its might to bend along with the force I am exerting on his limb. Bone crackles and his mouth goes agape as he is wracked with pain. My grip closes around the hand. There is tension as the bone tries everything to hold, but it is to no avail. It gives out. His hand jerks backward with a sharp distinct snap, followed by an animalistic wail of pain. My crowd explodes into whoops and hollers. The pirate leaps away, clutching at a dangling hand now only barely connected to his forearm.

As he raises his head away from his wound, I elbow him in the face and he collapses to the ground, raising his mutilated arm in defense. Some of the pirates struggle to writhe out of their chains, but they can't get free. Blood flows like a fountain from the nose of the kid. The crowd laughs as he attempts to crawl for the edge of the ship, yet I descend on him before he can do so.

With a heavy blow of my metallic arm, I split his leg in half at the thigh; the lower half of his ruined leg springs upward in an unnatural fashion. More wailing, more angry cursing from the pirates, more hollering from my men. The kid has stopped crawling now, holding onto the stump of his mutilated leg with his only good hand. I walk over and stomp his jaw with the heel of my heavy boot. Blood sprays onto the deck and flows into a puddle. Before he can spit out his broken teeth, I follow through with another kick, then another, and another—a pendulum in a way.

He sobs like a woman in that annoying tongue, white eyes bulging against a canvas of crimson. I raise my foot high and bring it down with all my weight onto the kid's head. A final satisfying crunch. My boot sinks into brain matter before I lift it out. Blood has stained my soles. The kid goes limp. His arms collapse onto the floor, outstretched and broken. That face is entirely concave. The skull is a bowl of blood and flesh, his features no longer recognizable.

His comrades go quiet, except one who begins to sob deeply. I grab the tattered scruff of the kid's shirt, and heave the limp body toward the edge of the ship.

"He wanted to escape, everyone. So let's allow him to escape." I announce in a theatrical manner, tossing the mangled mess over the edge of the ship. It falls like a stone into the cloud of dust. Out of sight.

As I turn around I notice Ulric has come back to join us after delivering his little friend to the holding cell. The men around him hold up knives and guns in celebration of the kill, yet my brother simply watches me. I wonder what is going on inside that helmet.

He walks over to me, keeping his voice down low.

"What the hell was that?" he asks.

"It's called retribution," I hiss, wiping off the blood from my armor.

"Aryans aren't supposed to be capable of that. He was a kid."

"Who attacked us. Who attacked Aryans."

"So you act like a bloodthirsty savage? How can you be capable of doing that? We shouldn't be able to do that as civilized people."

"They are savages. They did this to our own kind. Step aside."

"We shouldn't stoop to their level," Ulric whispers to me.

"You don't know how things are on this ship. This is how we deal with enemies."

"Deal with enemies? You did something similar to that German girl in a bar," he says.

"She was a thief, just like these four. This is how I deal with criminals."

"This is just a game to you, isn't it?" Ulric mutters in disgust. "This place is your personal playground to act how you want. Forget it." In a defeated fashion, he slinks through the confused crowd and disappears from sight.

First he says we should spare them for experiments, and next he says we should end them quickly. What the hell is going on with my brother? Before I can ponder this any longer the crowd chants for more justice to be done and I meet their demands, taking out the knife that I keep on my belt.

I analyze its beautiful golden finish on the handle. The detailed eagle and swastika that are engraved on it. It is long, serrated, and gorgeous, and I drive it into the neck of the closest pirate I see. This man, his head as barren as this desert, looks off distantly as his eyes begin to redden. He lets out a few quiet gargles before I pull the knife back out, and he collapses onto the floor. His two remaining comrades attempt to distance themselves from the ever-growing pool of blood. One appears to be in his thirties, and the other is as bruised as a fallen apple.

"This is what you have been doing to our people every day, every month, and every year since the Reclamation. You try your fucking best to attack us and now you try to cower when the same treatment is given to you? Pathetic," I hiss to the three still-living captives, kneeling over the convulsing body of the one I just stabbed. "Perhaps my brother is right, we shouldn't drag this out. We'll have all of you out of sight in no time."

"Let's have ourselves a sanding!" I laugh to the crowd, who immediately know what to do. They all rush toward the two remaining Scavengers and hoist them up. We all begin strolling away from the bow, toward the back of the ship.

"How are things up there, Volker?" I ask from inside my helmet.

"Everything is on course, sir. Since we sustained no damage from the attack, stupid bastards couldn't even get a hit, we're still on course to arrive at the Descent in three days. How much longer are you going to be playing with your food?" Volker says.

"We're going to sand them now," I announce.

"Damn, I never get to see those," Volker complains.

"Next time I'll let you do the theatrics," I joke.

I trail behind the mob dragging the struggling Scavengers. I breathe deeply and take this moment to watch the vast flat landscape we are leaving behind. Somewhere, a crashed aircraft remains, which will only be swept up by time.

Eventually, we all reach the stern. It is an area caked in sand. The air is thick from the cloud that trails behind us. It rises like a volcano erupting beneath our very feet. All of us with helmets don't quite mind, but the Scavengers begin to choke and cough from the dust-filled air. Their eyes water as particles fly into their eyes and open mouths.

It is time to begin.

"Get the ropes on them," I order. Two men bring out a long pair of old tattered ropes. Sandings are a long tradition in the Kiln. Being exposed to the elements is the ultimate torture. The sun becomes a welcome friend as it quickly cooks the skin and overheats the body. Like I said, an hour until death. Yet sailors over generations have found crafty ways to make that pain last far longer. It turns out that the best shade in this desert is the cloud we leave behind. It blocks the sun just enough that the heat doesn't cause instant death.

Say a man is thrown overboard with a rope tied to his legs. He's lowered with his back to the ground down to the desert floor, nicely under the safety of the cloud. It's important to lower the man just enough that he drags along the sand. The ship continues on its way, and he goes along with it. Now, sand is a coarse material. Millions of those little rocks rubbing against the skin can have a nasty effect. After days it can even begin to grind, and eat away at the flesh, strip it down to the muscle and finally...the bone. The crew can sometimes hear the screams and moans from the unfortunate victim. Those are always the best sounds. Often sandings are used for disobedient men, or for traitors to the Reich. In this case, a special sanding is now in order for the savages who attacked us.

"Tie them on their legs, make it nice and tight," I say, and it is done. The Scavengers attempt to bludgeon one of my men, but it only seems to hurt his hand when he strikes the armor.

"These men are a people of the desert," I announce, holding my hand out toward the two pirates being tied up at the legs. "I feel we should reunite them with it. What do you say, men?" A series of agreements permeate the crowd.

"Fantastic!" I say. "So let's begin."

One of the pirates quickly begins begging. He attempts to kneel and plead, his still-chained hands outstretched as a sign of obedience.

"I require a pistol," I order, and one of the men who captured the culprits leaps to fulfill my wish. I thank him and check the gun. It has a fine handle as well. It isn't gold like my knife, but the finish is very attractive. It will do nicely.

One pirate is still holding out his trembling hands, while the other has his head down in what I assume is prayer.

"Thank you for making this easy," I mock. "He has his hands right out. What a kind gentleman." The crowd laughs.

I walk to the side of the begging man, and hold out my pistol to his head. His arms defensively go to his face and I am annoyed.

"Somebody grab his arms," I demand. One of my crew forcefully jerks the pirate's hands away from his face. That's better.

I aim my pistol again to his head and take in the fear that the creature is displaying in this moment, the very end of his life. Only now does he truly understand how those innocents felt when his kind, perhaps even he himself, struck them down without mercy.

With a smooth motion, I aim away from the skull, and fire three rounds at his hands. They shatter upon the impact of the bullets, turning into a pulpy mess. The pirate lets out a shrill scream and flails about in agony.

"Now he can't untie the rope," I conclude in chuckling satisfaction. "Throw him over."

Two men lift the writhing pirate up by his shoulders and drag him to the edge of ship. The Scavenger has only enough time to glance down at the cloud behind him before his body is flung over the side. The rope tied to him is attached to a solid steel pole, conveniently located at the edge of the stern. Right now it is short enough for him not to fall directly to the ground below. That is too merciful. A sanding is not a short process.

He falls through the cloud, leaving a puff upward in his wake. The rope snaps straight and we hear the signal crack of bone even through the churn of the engine.

The last Scavenger seems not to take in the events around him. His head is still bowed. I assume he has accepted his fate. I slap his head and he raises his arms in defeat, still not looking me in the eye. Grabbing his face, I force him to look at my helmet, yet his eyes look up into the sky. Very well.

I shoot three more rounds into this one's pair of hands and order the men to throw him over as well. Without a scream or a cry, he goes over. Another snap is heard and then silence.

The men untie the ropes, loosen them up, and then retie them back up, allowing the (what I would hope are) alive pirates to be lowered into the desert below. With arms raised in celebration, we all cheer at the justice we have done. Deep down, I know that I am not truly happy with this experience. For a moment, however, I should try to enjoy it and not ruin the festivities with the knowledge that more of them are on the edges of the Reich, waiting to strike.

Masihuin

What a fucking disgrace. Ulric, the S.S. Knight, is conversing with the Scavenger. Or, as he puts it, "interrogating." It is not an interrogation. Interrogation requires pain. It requires that the prisoner suffer and spill out all they know, unless they spill all they have. I've gone down to the holding cell in the last few days when he wasn't there. I did not see any new bruises or cuts on that ragged old body.

How can this kid tell me that I am not an ideal Aryan, and yet willingly spare an enemy of the Reich? As I sit here in my bed, I am unable to sleep. His audacity of a few days ago continues to slap me in the face. What is in that book he is reading? Surely Hitler spoke of what we must do to our enemies, how we must defend our people. I don't remember him ever talking about what way to do so.

Eventually, sleep just does not come to me and I give up. As I roll myself out of bed and put on my things, I decide that I need to confront Ulric about what he did a few days ago.

With just a short walk through the hallway I reach his door and knock three times. I wait. Nothing. I knock again and there is nothing. Why is he not in his room at night? A thought manifests itself. He's in the holding cell.

I march on, descending a flight of stairs. The prison quarters are on the lowest level of the ship.

Down here, you can hear the gravel and sand clinking against the bottom. As I turn a corner I stop, recognizing one of the voices bouncing off the walls as being distinctly Ulric's.

When I walk into the room, I spot my brother sitting on a stool—the Scavenger sits on the other side of the cage. They are talking. The Scavenger is the first to recognize me and his head goes down to his knees. Ulric, in response, shifts his head toward me. His face is expressionless.

"What are you doing?" I quietly ask, moving closer to the scene.

"Interrogating," Ulric replies in a dull voice.

"Doesn't appear like interrogating, it seems more like a conversation," I retort, attempting to hold back anger.

"Well it's not," he denies. "If you're so paranoid that I'm fraternizing with the enemy, you are welcome to join me."

"I'm not the paranoid one," I correct him. "I'm concerned for you. We don't want anyone thinking you're being merciful toward them." I point to the old man curled up at the other edge of the cage.

"Anything other than smashing their face in with your boot is considered mercy...," Ulric mutters. "I don't think your lot has the best opinion on the subject."

"Why have you gone soft on them?" I accuse.

Ulric puts his hands to his beard in the same fashion he always does, deep in concentration. We sit quietly for a few seconds, the shaken old man watching the charade in puzzlement.

"I haven't," he says. "I am just acting like a regular, civilized Aryan. Apparently it's a bit of a culture shock to see that down here. What I want...is results. A Scavenger isn't useful to me dead. We could get good information from him. Learn about what they think...if they think. So, do you want to join me?"

I focus my attention on another seat in the room. I pick it up and place it next to him. We bring our seats closer to the old man sitting with legs crossed in the corner of the cell. Tattered black robes cover most of his small frame. His beard has become disheveled after days in this cell, yet his composure is surely anything but. In fact, he sits in front of us calm and collected.

"This is Haroun," Ulric says, pointing to the man. The fact that he even knows his name catches me off guard.

"You know his name?" I ask, bewildered. "How long have you been talking to him?"

"A few days. We've actually been able to converse a lot about the Kiln and what it means for both of our people. Apparently, he is from a place of great stone mountains. He says they were built by man. You know...Egypt."

I brush this little fact off, and immediately want to know one answer. "That's nice," I say to Ulric. "Did you ask him why the Jews attack us?"

"Scavenger," I yell at the old man. "You are a Jew. A pest. Why do you attack our people?"

"Jew?" he says in a puzzled, raspy voice. It was as if the sand itself was attempting to speak. Grating and ancient. "Jew...Jew...," he mutters to himself.

"Yes, that is what you are. A Jew," I hiss.

"Oh! I know what that is, I read it one of your books," the Scavenger exclaims in discovery. "No, no, in my home...we call... them Alyahudi. They...wear...similar clothing...to pictures...."

Ulric and I pause, taking in what he just said.

"What do you mean 'call them?' " Ulric asks. "You are them. You are Alyahudi."

This is met with a laugh from the old man sitting on the floor. He raises his arms in delight and I am tempted to stab them with the knife.

"I am not Alyahudi...or as you call them...Jews," he chuckles.

"He's lying." I conclude. "He thinks we'll set him free if he isn't a Jew."

"Then, what are you?" Ulric asks, ignoring my statement. What is he doing?

The old man reaches into his black robe, and pulls out a symbol, a small metal object attached to his necklace.

"I am what we call...Masihuin," he concludes, holding out the necklace. "We...do not follow...the Jews religion...I'm...trying to think...of German...word for it..."

I crouch down and take a look at the necklace. It's a cross. My mind goes blank. How did this savage get ahold of a symbol of the Reich?

"No," I dismiss. "You are not that different from them because of this. He has the same symbol too."

I point to the broad German cross plastered onto Ulric's armor. The German cross was a symbol that predated even the Reclamation. One of the few surviving relics of the first Aryans. It's an offense for this old creep to say he is similar. I analyze the gold symbol. It's thick like the German cross, but covered in elaborate engravings. I reach out and run my hand across the circle at the center.

"Let me continue, Ansel," Ulric says behind me. My mind blank, I simply get up and sit back on the chair.

"How do Masihuin and Jews differ then? Aren't you racially the same?" Ulric says.

"Oh, no...Jews...are lighter skinned...just a bit darker than you...they are not...native to my land...they are from...across old sea," Haroun says. "But our...disagreements...are more on...faith. Jews not... believe...that the Savior died...for us."

"So the Savior was like a warrior then? Died in battle?" Ulric asks.

"No...Savior...gave himself up...as sacrifice."

"No killing?" I ask.

"Of course not," Haroun denounces, almost offended. "He was... not...a man...of violence."

"This is ridiculous, Ulric, come on," I scoff.

"Did he die for your people? Your race?" Ulric pesters.

"No...he died for all...even you."

"Why are we messing with this sort of stuff, Ulric?" I ask, belligerent. "How can we trust anything he says?"

"We can't...and we aren't. But I still want to know what he is going on about. You know I'm curious."

"Yes and stupid," I say. "So, your friends were Jews then? The ones we killed."

"Killed?" the man says, genuinely surprised. "You...killed them?"

"Yep, every single one," I laugh. The man's eyes begin to water and he looks at the floor.

"Stop it, Ansel, he is going to shut down," Ulric demands.

"Good," I say. "So we can be done with this. You wanted to smash that disc artifact because it was dangerous, yet here we are talking to a Scavenger who probably planted ones like it."

"Why were you and your friends out there?" I demand loudly in the direction of the old creature. "Why did you attack us?"

The man wiped off his tears and collected himself again, straightening out his back and clutching the cross.

"I...did...not...attack you. You...killed those who attacked you," he whimpers.

"What do you mean?" Ulric asks.

"I came along...to ask for Allah's protection. I did...not fire a gun at your...ship." Harroun stutters out. He raises up the cross and does a few strange hand signs.

"Allah. What is an Allah?" I ask.

"Allah is the...Creator...of all things...he sacrificed his...only son for us. That...is what my...people believe," Haroun preaches. He takes out a thick novel, crumbling just like himself and places it into Ulric's hand.

"It is in Greek," Haroun says. "We have...a community...of them... in...my city...history tells us...they came...as the sea...began to wither. We...band...together for...protection from...the caliphate—"

"Wait, wait, you have history before the Reclamation?" Ulric asks.

"Before you get into this, I want to know why his friends attacked us. Even if he said he didn't," I butt in. "Why did your friends attack us? Why do your people attack us?"

"My people...do not attack...of our own power...we are...forced—"

"By the Jews?" Ulric says.

"No, no Jews are...tiny...minority...maybe only one thousand...we... are forced by caliphate."

"What is caliphate?"

"Muslim...state...control...everything...south of...big...towers to the seas."

He uses his arms to form the shape of a crescent. That is a Jew symbol. I've seen it flying on Scavenger vessels before, and on Eagle Nests overtaken by raiders.

"Those are Jews," Ulric says, which is met with a headshake.

"No...no...they...believe in Allah as well...like me and Jews...but believe...prophet instead...of son of Allah."

My head spins in the confusion, I lost my patience five minutes ago.

"They...control...all not Muslims...and force us...to fight along in their raids...against towers...I come along...to give blessings for those...Masihuin on front lines. Most along with...Muslims...killed in your blasts...me and some...fled to aircraft...to escape."

"So what do the Jews do?" I ask.

"Jews...are...not...even anything...they...are...only two or three... villages far east from my home. They...are...not...really...even thought...about."

"So what are you people then if you are not Jews?"

"We are Alearab," he says. "Our...people line the...great basin...what used...to be...the sea...the sea your...people took away."

"Now, wait a second," Ulric cuts in. "We took away the sea for the good of the world. For peace."

"Peace?" Haroun questions. "My people...tell how...when the sea disappeared...chaos reigned...children starved...entire communities vanished...wars erupted...perhaps it was peace for you...but it destroyed us."

"Your region has always been at war," Ulric says, "don't blame that on us."

The old man laughs once more.

"All regions have been...at war...that is what...man does...but...when the sea went away...it was not...just war...it was genocide against... my people...genocide and anarchy for all people...over any water that was left...but in the end...it did not matter...as we were left to the sand...now we barely survive...you ask why they raid your towers...it is because war is all they know...."

"Was raping and killing our people all your people know too?" I mutter, my frustration growing.

Haroun looks at me and his head sinks into his lap.

"Barbarity is...what the caliphate has brought us...what they do to... your people...they do to ours all the time...your dams brought the caliphate...that...symbol..." Haroun points to the swastika on Ulric, "has brought the caliphate on us...you destroyed...our way of life... thousands of years ago. Just...as our soul died...you...killed...your own soul...you abandoned the son of Allah...abandoned the soul of Europe...gave into...immorality...and arrogance...in the end...all of us...wither like the sea...now both our people...rot in the desert."

"What bullshit. The desert is the best thing to happen to me. The dams saved Europe. Why are we still listening to this shit?"

"The dams saved Europe," Ulric says. "Our people fought a horrendous war over resources and power. Adolf Hitler, the Eternal Führer, constructed the Atlantropan dams to bring an era of peace. All united under the Reich soon after, that was the real soul of Europe. There hasn't been fighting between our people since. The desert was a side effect, but it wasn't like we could just destroy what brought us all together. The dams create energy for all Europeans. They keep the peace."

"Dams destroy...both souls...you both are product of desert... product of the evil that has...corrupted...your people...corrupted my people...the raids are because of those vile dams...you are a result of those dams."

I take out my knife but before I can reach for the calm man, a voice blares in my headset.

"*Captain, you are needed urgently on the Bridge.*"

Ulric and I look at each other. I quickly get up and begin sprinting toward the deck. Once there, as I put my helmet back on and peer over the side, I take in the full view of something else. It's another ship.

Reinforcements

It couldn't be. We were all looking out of the window, silent.

"What the hell is that?" Witzel asks. Nobody responds. We all knew perfectly well what it was. It was another ship, and one so close to the other one. Why were they so close to each other?

"It's a damn hunter pack," I conclude. "They're scouting out this area for easy pickings."

"Fuck," Volker responds, running his hands through his hair.

I go to the radio again for confirmation, just to make sure that this isn't one of our ships. "*Howling Dark* to Eagle Nest #13, do you have any friendly vessels in the area?" I ask into the radio. Flames from the downed smaller enemy ship flicker in the distance. The familiar crackling of radio silence follows as the female voice once again confirms, "No, *Howling Dark,* you are the only vessel in the area."

Of course. I hang up communications with the Eagle Nest and switch to our deck down below.

"Status on the fire," I ask.

"Doesn't seem to be much damage, sir," a voice responds. "We doused the fire and it looks like it just needs some patchwork. No major hull damage."

I hang up.

"Alright," I announce to the Bridge crew. "I say, since we've probably already been spotted, we should start the festivities off first."

Everyone nods in agreement, even a shaken Ulric, and Volker turns the ship. Once again it careens, this time into the center of the dissipating storm, right toward our new arrival.

"Focus our main guns onto them, and fire when we are in range," I order. As the orange fog evaporates to reveal the clear blue sky of the Kiln, the Scavenger vessel becomes fully revealed. It is perhaps a kilometer or so away, yet the striking golden chassis of its hull is in full view. It glimmers like a gold coin left on a clean sidewalk in Germania. Stealth was never really the Scavengers' tactic, which is why this ambush was so unexpected. Guess that was why they relied on using the dust storm for cover.

As we come closer, the ship begins to shine brighter as the sun reflects off its turning body. They have noticed we are careening for them. Looks like we're in for a match.

"We're in range, sir," Witzel confirms, and I nod my head.

"Open fire with the main cannons," I state, still glaring at the obnoxious shining beacon against everything the Reich stands for. I've heard reports of when these ships would form fleets and attempt to attack the Nests. The attacks would usually always fail, but it was said there was nothing quite like seeing a couple dozen of those gleaming vessels barreling toward an innocent Nest.

The large silver cannons at the front of the deck aim themselves toward the distant golden ship and explode into a puff of black smoke and flames. Our ship rocks backward just slightly from the momentum, yet we push forward. With the storm now in our wake, a fully clear arena has been realized. On this white landscape there is only our ship and theirs.

White sand rises as the rounds splash around the Scavenger ship. One, two, three, yet there is no fire, and the ship carries on.

Smoke rises quickly from the enemy ship; yet it isn't because of our rounds. They are retaliating. We don't alter our course. We need to get in better range, for now it will simply be a game of who can connect the first shot, and Scavengers rarely are the ones to connect first.

There is a screech, followed by a deep thump. The ground to our port side explodes and sand splatters down onto the deck. Another round hurls right above the ship, missing it entirely. Those were pitiful shots.

Ulric sits in his chair, fidgeting. I know that he wants nothing more than to press a button and obliterate the ship from the air, yet I'm confident we won't need that. This is a match, and I set the rules.

The rules are that this ship will only need the weapons it brought with it.

Half a kilometer away now. I can begin to make out the spirals that jut upward on the gold ship. They're much like the towers on the *Howling Dark*; however, they are more like tentpoles. They hold up a large canopy of white and orange. All Scavenger ships have canopies. People theorize this is for shade, but I believe it's mostly for camouflage. Not camouflage from people on the ground—they paint their ships gold so that's out of the question—but camouflage from satellites.

The Reich controls space. Aegir Drops, colonies on other worlds, all of that. The most technological civilization on Earth which can bomb people from beyond the atmosphere, and yet, because of those damn canopies, the Scavenger ships blend right into the vast desert. We are practically blind to when a raid will show up to an Eagle Nest on the border until it is already there. Even with all of our technology, we are bested by a well-colored rug.

We fire another volley. The front of the golden ship opens up as a round slams right into it. An eruption of flames and metal bits scatter out into the white ground below. However, the ship continues moving. Another round grazes the side but plops right outside. The third misses entirely.

They're coming closer.

"How many more rounds do we have in those main guns?" I ask Volker.

"We have enough for two more volleys, sir," he responds.

"Fuck," I curse under my breath, "really wish we could bring more ammunition on the journey."

"We all do, sir," Witzel replies.

"Why can't you have more ammunition?" Ulric asks me.

"Because we don't have enough storage. We need room for the cargo, food, water, other supplies, and so ammunition is purely for defensive purposes," I answer, putting my hand to my brow.

"So why can't I just call in the Aegir Drop then?" he insists.

"Because we haven't run out of ammo yet, now have we?"

More rounds go screeching over our heads. One lands to our starboard side, rocking the ship and me along with it. The second hits right in front of the ship and we travel through smoke and the falling sand.

"Have the rounds been loaded yet?" I ask.

"Almost," Volker replies, looking over the dashboard.

"How often does this happen?" Ulric asks, looking at the glinting ship traveling ever closer.

"Every few trips or so, nothing to worry about," I reassure.

"It's loaded, sir, ready to fire on your say," Witzel confirms.

I hold my hand up, keeping my eyes on the ship. It's coming so close that the details on the bow are becoming distinguishable. Intricate patterns of diamonds and curves cover the rusting golden husk. Green flags flutter on the bowsprit.

"Fire," I mutter.

In a certain, explosive roar, more black smoke cascades out of the cannons, sending the rounds flying across the desert. Not even a second later, one of them slices into the canopy. The white tarp shreds apart from the impact and flies into the air, left behind in the vessel's wake. Yet there is no explosion. Another plunges into the side and combusts in a cloud of fire. The ship still continues onward. The third plummets in front of the bow, creating a cloud of dust which the ship sails right through.

It was hit but isn't going down.

They respond in kind, yet their rounds land around us as well. They are too close now to use the main cannons. We're almost face-to-face. They are only a couple hundred meters from us now. Quarter of a kilometer now.

"Stop," I order. "We need to salvage the last rounds. Turn us around. We're going to use the side cannons."

"Side cannons?" Ulric yells, "Let me just use the Drop!"

"Get back in your seat and let us handle this!" I erupt in a belligerent yell. "Our sides are far better protected than theirs. They can't penetrate our armor. There is no better plan."

"There is a better plan. Let me do my job."

"And let me do mine! We don't need the Drop. We're protected."

"You can't be certain of that! This isn't about your fucking ego!"

"I can be certain I don't need a space savior to do my duty. And I'm certain I don't need you lecturing me. That was not a part of the agreement. I will destroy that book if you are insubordinate one more time. I am perfectly capable of destroying a Scavenger ship by my own hand and I don't need a strike from the heavens to do it."

"You are going to get us killed because of this egotistical bullshit," he retorts.

Ulric goes toppling backward as my fist connects with the side of his cheek. Volker and Witzel watch wide-eyed as my brother lands squarely on the metal floor. I turn to them and bark.

"We're going to fire at them! Turn this fucking vessel," I command, my blood becoming as hot as the desert outside, sweat trickles down my forehead.

"Sir," Witzel says, "I think he's right. We should just call in the Drop."

"You've never been uncertain of that before, Witzel," I yell. "Only reason I'm not throwing him overboard is because he's my brother. Don't tempt me."

"Sir...."

The *Howling Dark* spins around, its main cannons facing away and its side cannons now facing the golden ship starboard. The

Scavengers are barreling toward us. I can't let them get any closer, and I can't let them chase us.

I don't need a fucking Drop to do the job of a competent captain. Using my binoculars, I can see the bodies of the hundred or so savages scurrying about on the golden vessel. They are all covered in brown and red rags with makeshift metal slats covering any exposed skin. Even Scavengers have makeshift armor.

Their deck is dirtied and rusted. Large spindles that now hold only tattered remains of their ruined canopy spring out of the deck. Tiny cracks ring out, it's almost like rocks are being thrown at the ship. Men on our deck duck and scramble about. The ship is still far smaller than our own; I would guess it goes right up to the treads.

They're shooting at us. My men begin retaliating in kind. Five hundred meters. There is an open fire-fight between our two vessels. Islands in a sea of death. We have the elevation advantage, being able to shoot down at them.

One of my men stiffens up and collapses onto the floor. More rally behind him, and take cover among the cargo and walled sides of the ship.

Bullets zip and crack, bouncing off of the metallic tower as we loom over the golden ship. Some of the Scavengers keel over as they are hit by our better marksmen. It's a war zone. The men on the side guns remain composed, however, ducked down and ready for the word. I just need their ship to get a tad closer so we can get the perfect shot.

"Sir, if we don't fire now...," Volker says.

"Wait," I emphasize. "We only have one chance at this."

"They're going to ram into us."

"Just...a few more...."

I see out of the corner of my eye that Ulric is dusting himself off.

"You're mad," he mutters. "If we die, it's on your hands."

"If our Reich engineering doesn't save us, and we die, we die honorably."

"Why do you refuse to allow me to call it in?"

"Because I'm not a coward."

"Coward?!"

Four hundred meters. Three hundred... Two hundred...

"Fire," I mutter.

The cannons sound and our ship is lifted up momentarily on its side. A plume of smoke overtakes the Bridge's windows, followed by the unmistakable cry of steel shattering apart. All on the Bridge are tossed into the air and fall back down with a thud. I collect myself quickly and gaze out the window.

Through the smoke, a warm glow flickers. The distinct shockwave of an expanding explosion graces my ears. As the fog dissipates, everything is revealed. I look on to the Scavenger vessel. One of the spindles has collapsed into a canyon that has now been carved into the middle of the vessel. It is practically split in half by the barrage. Somehow the ship is still moving on its treads, despite the inferno raging on it. Scavenger bodies tumble into the hole, and off the ship on fire. Black smoke churns across the deck as the ship continues on, a husk of its former self.

"Sir," Volker says quietly.

"We did it," I respond.

"We've taken damage."

I put down the binoculars to see our deck riddled with holes and caked with flames. Blood has been splattered amongst the crumpled bodies of men still holding their weapons. I can't see the bowsprit. All there is is a short metal stick instead of the long, jutting sword.

Long ravines are carved deep into the metal where the Scavenger's rounds skimmed past. My heart sinks. They did penetrate. At least, on the deck they did.

"What is the damage?" I ask, blankly.

Volker looks over the numerous blinking alerts.

"We took some damage in the engine room, the bow deck is heavily damaged, we lost the bowsprit, and...."

"And what?"

"And it seems like they damaged one of the treads."

"How? They have weak cannons...how the hell did they hurt the treads?"

"Lucky shot, I suppose."

"They were missing all those shots before."

"I don't know what to say, sir."

"Fucking...will it hold?"

"I don't know, sir...they are supposed to handle anything, even enemy fire...I haven't dealt with something like this before."

"It's coming...," Ulric mutters, touching a cheek now turning purple.

I let out a yell in frustration.

"Fire again!" I order.

"No need," Ulric says.

I turn to see him speaking into a small radio. He is looking at the dashboard with our coordinates, is whispering something about his Knighthood, and then...he says, "Aegir."

More rounds fly past our tower. The fucking ship is still not dead. My heart simply feels empty, and my mind is wrapped in nothing but the deep well of defeat.

"I'm sorry," Ulric tells me quietly. "I know you wanted it to go differently."

"Drowned like a fish, I suppose," I mutter, running my hands across my sweating face.

Above our heads, I hear a distinct boom. It isn't the sound of a round flying past our head. The roar only gets louder, deeper, more distinct, as if something was falling toward us.

One hundred meters.

I look outside as the towering blazing ship still moves with all its strength toward us. Scavengers fall off the side of it, and yet it's not stopping. And then, it does.

In a moment, it explodes into a puff of sand and smoke. We are all lifted off our feet once more, and the windows around us shatter. Sand blasts into the Bridge along with the scalding Kiln air. The entire ship rocks to one side, almost feeling like it will tip over, yet instead it flops back on two treads with a mighty crunch.

I spit up blood as I lift myself up on the floor littered with broken glass. Howling winds surround me as I feel my bare skin begin to burn. I crawl slowly to pick up my helmet on the other side of the room, gasping for proper air. On my stomach, I place my helmet onto my head. The satisfactory pressurized heave of the suit releases fresh, breathable, and cold air into my lungs. Lying there for a second, I take in my surroundings.

Ulric is lying face down across the room. His helmet...where is his helmet? I pull myself up and stumble around to look for it. I see it tossed near a knocked-over shelf.

I take Ulric's helmet and quickly place it onto his body. His eyes open.

"I think the blast made me black out for a sec," he groans, stretching his arms. "Did it work? Did the Aegir Drop do the job?"

I put out my hand and pull him up. We look at the crumpled-up heap of metal, now consumed by a mountain of sand. There is now a deep crater in the flat landscape.

"Yeah...it did the job," I reply in a soft, gasping tone.

Walking over to Volker, I pick him up. He extends a weak knee to prop himself up, clutching at a bleeding wound on his face.

"I took glass to the face," he sputters, coughing up a glob of blood.

"We'll get you a Med-Kit," I comfort. "Ulric, how is Witzel?"

"Ansel, I...," Ulric says, standing over the collapsed body of a kid his age. "It's not good."

I prop Volker onto a chair and give him one of my cloths to stop the bleeding, then make my way to the still unconscious Witzel, face down in a pool of crimson. With a gloved hand I turn the kid over and close my eyes slowly in disappointment. Disappointment at myself for letting this happen.

When I open them I see Witzel, his blue pupils clashing with bloodshot irises. A large shard of glass had lodged itself directly into his neck. The blood is pouring like thick syrup out of his half-open mouth and punctured windpipe. He looks at me wide-eyed, gargles a few words, then stares upward unmoving.

Honor in Death

The ship is damaged. We patched it up the best we could, but there wasn't much we could do with the resources we have out here. We'll need to get to an Eagle Nest for repairs, and it's at least thirty kilometers away. The *Howling Dark* is limping its way to safety.

We lost nine men. Two to gunshots. Six to cannon fire. One to broken glass. Ulric, Volker, and I stand in the empty husk of the Bridge. The day is clear, so only a little bit of sand comes through—even so, we still need to wear our armor and helmets to stay safe. Volker was able to get patched up. We buried the dead, including Witzel, in the desert, placing tokens with swastikas on top of the graves. From the environment of the crew, none of them blamed me for what happened.

It was just the nature of the Kiln, and the nature of the Scavengers. Our friends died serving the Reich, and as the Eternal Führer preached, that is the most noble death any of us could hope for. They all died heroes—but deep down, I know they didn't need to die like that.

I've done that same maneuver dozens of times. Sure, it is risky, but it always came with a big reward as well. The shots from the main cannons were missing. They have a narrower range than the side cannons. It was meant to be one decisive blow, and it has worked before. Yet instead of celebrating victoriously while sailing away from the wreckage of our enemies, I watched over my men's burials in this land of salt and sand.

With the tread damaged, nobody knows how long we have until it gives in. For now, we simply take it slowly and delicately. It may give out at any second, or it may not. For now, I stand here on the Bridge, in my armor, staring out through an open window, anticipating the clunk of the tread's final rotation.

I pick up the radio to prepare for emergency pick-up from the nearest Nest in case our ship is stranded. I click the button, but there is no soft white noise. I click it again, and then again. Then I try my helmet. Nothing.

"I'm not getting any signal from outside the ship," I tell Volker.

"What do you mean? I can hear you fine through the helmet intercom," Volker replies.

"Yeah, but the helmets work on a limited range. I'm trying to use long range and it isn't working. I think our long-range communications are damaged."

"Fuck. I'll send somebody down on the deck to check," Volker replies. He turns around and says through the short-range radio, "Hey, go check the long-range communication rod see if it's there. We can't get signal outside the ship."

We stand in silence, awaiting a response.

"They knew what they signed up for," Volker responds in a reassuring tone. "This is the Kiln. Fuck, every boy in the Reich dreams of fighting against the Scavengers. When we get back, they will be remembered for what they did today. We stopped two ships from getting further north...that's something."

"I suppose."

"Witzel was a good officer."

"He was. The last thing I said to him was I was going to throw him overboard...all because he wanted me to call in the Drop."

"I didn't want the Drop called in either," Volker admits, "it feels... so against...what Hitler stood for. About a noble battle. Feels like it robs something from defending the race...you know."

"I never once had an Aegir Drop called in, not once...we always found a way to get out of tough situations."

"I wonder why this time was different."

"When you do something so much, you eventually stop seeing the danger in it, I suppose."

"You forget how dangerous the Kiln really is. I get that."

"You do?"

"Well...not personally. But I'm not Captain. Captains need to have that personality—First Officers don't. We're the ones that keep that stupidity in check."

I chuckle. "I suppose you're right. Where were you two hours ago?"

"Following orders the best I could."

It's noon by now. The sun is at its highest and strongest. This metal cabin is becoming a furnace without the safety of the windows. Even under my armor, I can still feel the creeping kiss of the smoldering desert air. Volker excuses himself and retreats underneath the deck to tend to his wounds again, and probably to escape the heat too, leaving just Ulric and I alone overlooking a white and orange plain.

"I fought to retake Eagle Nests when I was seventeen," I reflect. "Didn't think anything of it. Sure it was dangerous. I lost my arm, shook it off, kept going. This is my element. I command this element. The desert and sand, and facing off any threat that gets in my way. After years...the danger just becomes the average."

"Remember the family cottage in Bavaria? We went there every summer," Ulric remarks, his tone shifting.

"Yeah, Father wanted me around all the time but I went off sometimes to fuck the local girls," I say.

"That's where you went?" Ulric asks.

"Oh? Oh yeah, you were too young to know that."

"Anyway, there was always this cliffside I would climb, and I never thought it was dangerous...until I slipped. I didn't fall or anything, but it was that jolt—your heart racing when you realize that you're not on flat ground. Sometimes we forget and it takes a slip to bring perspective," he explains.

"Hell of a slip this was," I mutter.

We continue on in silence, watching the distant blurry pillars rising on the horizon. They aren't ships, they are towers. The first

Eagle Nests that we've seen on this journey. Eagle Nest #13. It appears so close, yet I don't know if we will make it.

"Father always had a good way of putting things in perspective," I reminisce. "You get that from him. Apologies about the hit earlier." I point to the part of his helmet that I assume his cheek is under.

"You get the temper from Mother," he says. "And the stubbornness."

"Oh yeah, she was really stubborn about me going to a good university. 'Don't go into the military,' she said. 'It won't do any good for you.' Silly her though, I got a metallic arm out of it." I joke, holding up my rusting arm.

"She forced me to go into university," Ulric flatly admits. It catches me by surprise.

"What? I thought you were a scholar and wanted to study the Reich history, and all that."

"I do. But I kinda wanted to serve first, you know? You were already deployed into the Kiln. Kinda looked up to that, wanted to be like that. The Eternal Führer always wrote about fighting for our people."

"He talked about serving the people as well," I explain. "And you are a Knight, a descendant from his original guard—if that isn't serving, I don't know what is."

"Right," Ulric agrees. "This should be a dream come true."

"And it isn't?"

"It's...it's not what I thought it'd be like. Maybe I just envisioned the rest of the Reich like Germania. I knew that the Kiln was dangerous, but...."

"But what?"

"I guess I just imagined it'd be different."

"Different how?"

"When I first envisioned calling down an Aegir Drop, I thought it would be this glorious moment. The feeling you get when you've served, did something. Yet it wasn't out of glory, it was out of desperation. The blast hurt our own...even if it saved us. Like, the salvation ended up harming everyone on both sides, even if we survived."

"What are you getting at?"

"We've always been taught the dams are good because they give us endless energy, and stopped us from going to war again. And the dams are good, don't get me wrong...they saved us. Yet at the same time, it still harms us...you know? The dams drained the sea... it took something away to prevent us from losing everything. Just like the Drop took away so we could be saved."

"The dams took away the water?"

"The water...something...I don't know if this Reich is what the Eternal Führer would have wanted. For us to still be fighting against Scavengers and defending our borders thousands of years after he is gone."

"You are the scholar, you'd know more than anyone here what he would have wanted. But I think he'd be happy to simply see the Aryans alive."

"He didn't just want the Aryans alive. He wanted his people, those that looked like him, with blond hair, blue eyes—this destined strong race—to thrive. This doesn't feel like thriving. It feels like we're straggling."

"He did say that we would struggle with the Scavengers, you know. Plagues can come back occasionally."

"I've always wondered why we can't just invade down south. Find the Scavengers and end this once and for all."

"You're asking the wrong person, Ulric. I always figured it was because it's better to protect our own borders."

"If I was Führer, we'd do things differently."

"I'm sure you would."

"I'd try to find the lost records before the Reclamation. Imagine seeing the actual faces of the original National Socialist leaders. Hitler, Goebbels, Göring, Himmler, Hess...they must have towered over the lesser Europeans like gods...with true Aryans being so rare. I wonder how out of place they felt."

"I would like to see what Germania looked like before it was Germania. I read somewhere it was called Berlo...Barlan..."

"Berlin."

"Ah yes, thank you. See I'm not a historian. Just know enough to get by."

There is a crackling on my helmet radio and a wispy voice comes through. It's Volker.

"Status on the long range communications, Volker." I ask urgently.

"Yes, sir," he responds, "there is a massive hole where they used to be. The entire relay is gone."

"Fuck," I curse. "Alright, come back up here. We need to get this thing to the Eagle Nest."

Volker cuts the radio, and I turn back to Ulric.

"Long range communication is down," I announce. "We can't get through to anybody outside the ship."

"So what now?" he asks.

"Now we're on our own."

I bring my hands to my helmet, and take a deep breath—squinting my eyes, wishing for this situation to end.

"Hell of a first journey into the Kiln, isn't it," I mutter to Ulric, my mouth contorting into a smile. Sometimes when situation gets bad, I can't help but find myself laughing at the preposterousness of the problem.

"If you would have just called in the—"

"Stop," I interrupt my brother.

"These is a tool we have at our disposal, I don't see how it isn't honorable," Ulric says.

"Do you feel like you really fought against those Scavengers?" I turn around and say, my voice becoming tense.

Ulric looks at me and pauses for a few seconds, stuttering out a response.

"Well...yes," he concludes. "My action brought down the steel rod and it struck down our enemies—it saved us."

"But you didn't personally do it yourself."

"Yes, I did," he defends, "I pressed the button, my action led to their ship exploding."

"It's not the same."

"How is it not?!"

"There is nothing like looking your enemy in the eye when you drive in that knife, or shoot that gun. The people who have ravaged the Aryans since time began. It's personal. It's real. It's how our ancestors did it."

"Perhaps I don't share the same views on protection of the race as you do."

"Perhaps you don't. You're the more intellectual type anyway."

"I told you that we needed to call in the Drop. You were too arrogant. You wanted to relive some battle fantasy, so you didn't even consider how you were putting us in danger."

"I have done that maneuver dozens of times before you even entered school, I don't need you lecturing me," I spit.

"You don't even feel guilty for what happened?"

"Of course I do!" I yell.

There is a pause. Ulric stares at me through his helmet. I slouch myself down onto a chair near the dashboard.

"Of course I do. I'm the Captain. This is my ship. Every death, I feel. I know..." I collect myself, putting my rusting arm on my knee and looking up at Ulric. "I know that we should have called in the Drop. But you have no idea how hard that was for me. It's like...like a clash between my survival, and glory...I feel like they are opposites."

"What do you mean?"

"Perhaps my glory in this desert is not achieved by surviving. Perhaps it's through death in battle. Like the Eternal Führer wanted."

"You aren't a grunt in the military anymore," Ulric flatly states. "You can't just die in combat. You can't send this ship into the fray like you're charging enemy guns. It's your duty to protect everyone on this ship. Protect me."

"I know."

"And protection means calling in any resources we need to keep the ship safe."

"I know," I repeat again, in a lowered, annoyed tone. "It doesn't mean I agree with it."

A loud crack rings out across the ship. Both of us are launched forward by the *Howling Dark*. I slam into the dashboard and Ulric topples into a wall. Then, not a second later, the ground slowly begins to tilt to the starboard side. The tread has broken and partially given away.

Ulric and I slowly lift ourselves to our feet. The wind was knocked out of me and so I struggle to breathe.

"You alright?" Ulric asks me.

I hold out a finger to him, while my other arm clutches at my stomach.

"I'm fine," I cough. "Just got hit in the chest."

We stumble around, attempting to maintain our stance. With the tread having partially given way, the ship is listing a few degrees. The other engine attempts to spin, rotating the vessel before I reach the dash and stop the movement. In a few seconds, the ship comes to a halt.

We are stuck. I peer out toward the Eagle Nest far away, its large towers sluggishly rising above the white desert. Taunting us.

Volker opens the door in a slow, delicate fashion, trying to maintain his balance. He meets Ulric and me, all of us understanding the dangerous situation we are in. The ship is trapped, and we have no communications with the outside world.

"We need to send for help," I tell him.

"Fantastic, that's what I was thinking. Because I don't feel like boiling alive in this sitting oven," he responds.

"So what do we do," Ulric asks me in a flat voice.

"We can't walk, it's too far," I theorize. "We have the Camels, however, and they certainly have enough fuel in them to get us to the Eagle Nest on the horizon."

"Does everyone take the Camels out of the ship?" Ulric says.

"Of course not," Volker says. "We still have the cargo, what if another Scavenger ship comes by?"

"It's just cargo. Are you willing to die for that?"

"There are weapons in those cargo crates as well," I butt in. "If they get ahold of those guns and ammunition, then who knows what damage they could do."

"Most of the men will need to stay here to defend it, or in case help comes," Volker states.

"Is there supposed to be another ship coming this way?" Ulric says.

"Not for at least two days," I state. "We still have the engines and cooling running, but I don't know if the ship's power can last that long."

"So somebody will have to make the trip. They have those tow ships in the Nest. They could drag the ship to safety," Volker says. "We can send somebody from the engine room, or maybe a guardsman."

My mind races as I think about the predicament we are in. It is a dangerous journey, crossing over in the Camels. Even if they were life rafts, they are still prone to breaking down and are not as sturdy as a full-treaded ship. I don't want to lose another sailor out here.

"I'll do it," I say. "I have friends at the Eagle Nest anyway who will recognize me and we can get help quicker. I'll go on the Camel."

"You're the Captain, sir," Volker insists. "You don't need to do this."

"I ordered the maneuver and the maneuver failed, this is my responsibility and so I'll go on the Camel to get help."

"I'll come with you," Ulric says.

"No," I reply. "You stay here with Volker and keep an eye on everything. Camels aren't safe."

"I'm not a child," Ulric argues. "When you were my age, you did far more dangerous things. You got your arm blown off."

"I wasn't a Knight, you are," I state, my temper flaring. I did not need to worry about my brother in the desert.

"You should really listen to your brother, Ulric," Volker insists. "Don't you need to do more research with the book anyway?"

"I'm not going to do research while worrying if Ansel is safe or not," Ulric states flatly. "I mean, we disagree but...still—I'm coming with you."

"I'm not having this conversation—you're staying. Volker prepare a Camel for me, I'm heading out in an hour," I repeat myself as

I stroll to the door and open it. I begin descending the staircase and hear footsteps behind me. "Stop it, Ulric, you don't know how dangerous it is out there," I state.

"And it's safer here?"

I turn around and look at him three steps above me.

"Yes, it is—we have guns, men, and most importantly, the closest thing to shelter in this desert. I need you here."

"And what if something happens? Am I supposed to wonder what happened to my brother?"

"If I don't come back by nightfall, they'll send another Camel to look for us. We have three. I won't be long."

Ulric takes off his helmet in the safety of the cool staircase, leans close to me and whispers, "I'm going. And I don't feel safe here anyway."

"What do you mean?"

"Your crew has been...treating me oddly...I think it's because I've been interrogating that Scavenger. They seem suspicious of me. It's stupid but I just don't feel comfortable if you leave me alone with them."

My mind races in confusion. Crew treating Ulric badly? What the fuck.

"What are you talking about? Who has been treating you badly? What are they doing? I want names."

"It's just a feeling of mine. You know that feeling in the pit of your stomach. That gut instinct something isn't right?"

"Far too well."

"I get that feeling every time I'm eating lunch, or walking the halls. They stare, and mutter. As if I'm a threat. I think they suspect me of siding with the Scavenger, or being sympathetic, I don't know, but after what happened with the Drop and Witzel I don't feel safe here. Please."

I look at my brother who has genuine concern on his face. My blood simmers as I contemplate how many feel that despicable way against a kid his age.

"Fine," I say. "When we are done with this journey and get back to Europe I want names, and will handle it. Let's just get this fixed."

"Thank you," he says.

We make our way down the stairs and underneath the deck. The Camels are housed in a large garage at the bottom of the ship. Men are rushing around us, attempting to fix anything they can and prepare for the long wait the *Howling Dark* will be in for. I study every face, thinking about which one could be planning something against Ulric. First, I damage my own ship, and now I might not even be able to trust my own crew.

Ulric and I walk through a doorway and a series of small hallways opens up into a large hangar. In front of me stands a line of three large orange vehicles held up by four wheels at either side. These were the Camels. Large compared to a human, yet small compared to anything we'd find out in the desert. Only a small light machine gun is propped on the top of the vehicle. They aren't meant for offense, to put it lightly.

"I need supplies for a day's journey to the Eagle Nest," I tell one of my men, dressed in a cloth of burgundy. "Food, weapons, water."

He nods and gathers other men to fetch the goods we need for our trek.

"When we go out there, you need to realize it won't be like being on this ship. This is an island in a sea," I tell Ulric.

"I know," he responds. "I can take the risks."

A man hurries through the doorway and enters the hangar. His helmet is off, revealing a very sweaty and disheveled First Officer Volker.

"Did you get the supplies?" Volker asks, out of breath. I assume he ran downstairs.

"The men are getting what we need for the journey right now," I say, examining the inside of the vast hangar. It's dark and musty, with only a few hanging lamps for light.

After a few minutes of waiting, a line of men begin to load up our Camel with the supplies we need. They all nod and go on their way.

"Are you sure you can hold everything down while I'm gone?" I ask Volker.

"More than I do already?" he laughs, and we shake hands. "Good luck out there you both," he says, shaking hands with Ulric as well.

"You as well, First Officer," I say.

Ulric and I walk into the open back of the Camel. It's a large transport meant to fit around ten people, so that means we'll have enough space.

"Are you sure you don't want any more men to come with you?" Volker asks me, standing outside the Camel.

"I don't want to risk anymore on this journey," I shout back. "This is my job." And I give him a smile before I press the button on the side wall which will begin closing the large hatch inside. As the Camel's hatch slowly shuts, Volker raises his arm outstretched in a salute.

"Sieg Heil," he calmly says.

"Sieg Heil," I repeat back.

The hatch rises over his face, and Volker disappears from view. A few seconds later, it closes with a deafening hiss, signifying that the cabin is pressurized and ready for travel. The lights around Ulric and me illuminate the grey steel box that is this vehicle. A row of seats line the edge of the walls, leading up to a cockpit with a wheel.

"I didn't want you to come on this with me," I tell Ulric, sitting. Then I get up, pace across the cabin to the seat at the front of the Camel, and prop myself neatly on it. Both hands wrap around the wheel as I take in the large windowed space that the front provides.

"I know," Ulric replies.

Alarms blare throughout the hangar. Red lights swirl around the great, large doors as they swing open. The bright light of the Kiln floods into my eyes as the sea of salt reveals itself. Dust and sand softly hug the steel portal with the whistling of wind.

My rusted arm presses a single large button on the dashboard of the Camel. The vehicle rumbles, as its engines roar to life, awoken from its slumber. Everything vibrates for a few seconds before settling down. I look to my left and see Volker, his hand raised in salute. I meet him with a nod, then turn back to the desert before me.

Ulric appears to my right, plopping himself down on the other seat. His face isn't laced with nervousness, but anticipation. The same anticipation as when he first came to this place. I didn't want Ulric here. Not just in this Camel, but in this land. I knew it was a terrible idea to include him on such a dangerous journey, but instead of listening to my gut, I suppressed it and allowed my little brother to be put in this situation.

If he weren't here, perhaps I'd just drive this Camel toward the Nest hoping, no, pleading that another Scavenger ship would find me. The *Howling Dark* would send another Camel. My men would survive without me.

My mind is tantalized by the image of me walking out into the desert one last time, gun in hand, ready to face down them all. Ulric says that seeing your opponent before you kill them doesn't matter, but I couldn't disagree more. There truly is nothing like it. I feel myself getting weaker every day. My breath labors, my skin wrinkles, my back aches. There is no greater curse than living past your prime.

Walking out into the desert to face down the Scavengers—that is the way I would want to go. I was robbed of that back in the military. I was robbed of a noble death. This rusted arm reminds me of it every time I wake up.

As I press on the pedal and the Camel moves forward, its tires hitting the desert ground with a graveling thump, my mind goes blank. All I think about is the pleasure of serving the Reich. The pleasure of dying with honor.

Yet now, with Ulric at my side, I cannot do that. He is better than I. Knows more about the Reich than I. He'd serve our race better than I ever could, even if we disagree. So as the Camel travels forth, away from the broken-down ship, I put aside in my mind the will for a glorifying death and focus on the dark towers up ahead.

The Kiln

The *Howling Dark* has disappeared past the rippling waves of hot desert air. The salt flats have evolved into the rougher terrain of sandy dunes. Looking forward, I can see the gradual curves transforming into larger hills. Camels are built for these steep inclines on the slippery slopes; however, it makes our journey far longer as a result.

Wind howls past the wide windows of the cockpit, carrying the dust cloud kicked up by the tires high up to the teal-blue skies. It is the only cloud in sight. With my foot on the pedal, I push the Camel to its limits. It bounces and sways as it collides with the rolling dunes. Thoughts in my head persist of another Scavenger ship arriving and finishing off the crew. They'd put up a reasonable fight with their still-operating guns but, without mobility, the ship would still be a sitting duck.

Those dark towers are growing. Tall spindling structures act as a beacon. Ulric sits next to me, looking out into the wide-open stretch of nothingness.

"I told you to let me call in the Drop," Ulric says again, his eyes staying focused on the dunes outside.

My fists clench around the steering wheel. I can feel my heart race faster, as this vehicle travels down the sandy desert. "I've done that maneuver before," I repeat.

"Yeah, I know," he says. "You've done everything down here before, but you know what happened? You got arrogant. You thought this place was your personal little sandpit and that you could do whatever you pleased, but you were wrong."

"Shut the fuck up," I curse, closing my eyes for just a second.

"What happened to you, Ansel?" Ulric mutters in disgust. "Is this what the Kiln does? Changes people? When...when was the last time you were even in Germania?"

I think about it, my eyes feel like they are coming out of my sockets. What kind of situation is this? The fucking stress is going to kill me. I feel like my heart is going to explode.

"Eight years ago," I say, feeling my head.

"In eight years you haven't even been up north?" Ulric asks me, to which I respond with a "yes." He puts his hands to his eyes. "This isn't how regular Europeans act. You disregard the laws. You harm other Aryans. You act like a bloodthirsty savage when confronted with the opportunity—"

"They attacked our ship—"

"It wasn't just the ship," he cuts me off. "You did it to that girl as well. This place is not what the Reich aspired to what it would be. It isn't like what Atlantropa was supposed to be at all. It's savage. It makes people savage. It made you savage, just admit it."

"Admit what?" I growl.

"Admit you only stay in this fucking desert because it's how you can escape the prying eye of the Reich you pretend to so dearly care about."

"I serve the Reich in my own way. I don't need you coming to the Kiln and telling me how I act in this desolate wasteland is bad," I mutter, keeping my eyes squarely on the dunes ahead of us. The towers of the Eagle Nest grow slowly the closer we get. Ulric doesn't respond, and we sit in silence for a few minutes.

"It's not even about the Reich," Ulric says. "After the last few days, I've just been thinking about what the point of this place even is. I'm sure we could come up with some other solution for renewable energy. Do we even need to depend on the dams anymore?"

"What?" I laugh. "You want to just flood the Kiln?"

"What's the point of this place?" Ulric argues, his voice rising. "If we got rid of the dams, it'd put a barrier between us and the rest of the world. We'd have the sea again and we wouldn't need to worry about Scavengers attacking our people."

"They could just get water vessels," I state. "Then they would actually attack Europe."

"So you're telling me the strongest nation on earth couldn't keep out a few pirates?" Ulric concludes with a laugh.

I sit in silence, running my hand through my hair in frustration. "We're talking about the fucking Atlantropan dams," I say, staring out the window. "You know how insane you sound?"

"Do you know how insane you've become?" Ulric retorts. "Why would we want to keep the Kiln? All it is...is an immoral place that corrupts normal Aryans. It's a burden on Europe, if anything...I can't believe I'm even saying that...."

"It's the best option we have right now," I say. "Without those dams, Europe wouldn't have energy. We'd fall right back into chaos like the Great War."

"I don't know...perhaps if we could figure out some better way to have renewable energy...we wouldn't need the dams," Ulric concludes. "Say we did."

"Say we did what?"

"Say we came up with a new form of renewable energy and didn't need the dams anymore. Europe is still stable and we don't need the Kiln. That's the perfect solution," he theorizes with an upraised, matter-of-fact finger.

I don't say anything for a few seconds. The temples of my head are beating. I can feel my chest heaving faster and faster. Why can I not breathe?

"I can't live up north," I admit. There is no response from Ulric. "I'd go insane...doing anything else. This ship, the Kiln with all the flaws...this is the only place I thrive...I can't go north again."

"We'd never have to fight the Scavengers in our territory again. All those men who just died, the people in the Eagle Nests over the years, they'd be safe. Witzel might be—"

"I enjoy it," I say flatly. "All of it. Killing those Scavenger fucks. Seeing them squirm as I cut them up limb by limb... after everything I've seen. It's makes life worth living. That's your answer."

Ulric looks at me with emotionless eyes before turning to look back out the window. There is no retort from him again. What were once distant and dark blurs have transformed into a forest of tall, spiraling towers sprouting out of the desert floor. As the ship slowly makes its way forward, the collection of buildings reveal themselves in all their glory. A traditional Eagle Nest colony often only has one tower. A wide, tree-like structure that stretches a kilometer-and-a-half into the air.

The thin towers ripple in the desert air. They are so close. As I gaze out toward them, suddenly everything goes bright...then silent. Pain shoots through my face. I clutch my eyes shut. I think I curse, but I'm not sure. Everything goes dark.

When I come to, there is wind. So much wind. As I attempt to open my eyes, I'm greeted with a blast of sandy desert air. My hand goes to my mouth, and when I look down, I see a palm covered in scarlet liquid. Fuck. Everything swirls about.

Feeling around, I can tell I'm no longer in my seat—everything is metal and steel. As my head swivels around, I notice that I'm lying by the side of the Camel. Why am I on the side of the Camel? To my right, I see glass scattered about the cabin, a remnant of the window that was once there. What hit us?

A pain swells in my chest and I violently cough. I suddenly realize I don't have my helmet on. The air gets knocked out of me as I continue to cough. My eyes catch something floating above me. Is that sand? No, it's moving too slow to be from the wind. It's smoke. Fire. The Camel is on fire. Forcing myself onto my side, I prop myself back up with my arms. Blood trickles off the side of my face and hits the metal wall.

Where is Ulric? My eyes open wide at the realization.

"Ulric...," I cough, continuing to dry-heave, "Ulric...."

A moan radiates throughout the vehicle. It's to my right, in the cockpit. Still in a daze, I force myself up and look into the shotgun seat. Ulric sits, slumped over in his chair. His face is speckled with bits of glass and blood cakes his face. His helmet got knocked off as well. My hands run over his chest and neck. There is no large piece. He didn't end up like Witzel.

He's still breathing as well. I tap his face a few times, calling his name. Eventually he comes to, and his eyes spring open, followed by a loud gasp.

"Ansel!" he exclaims, his arms clutching at his chest. "What...what the fuck...happened?"

"I don't know," I answer back. "I think we hit something...."

He swivels his head around, and the full extent of our situation comes to him too.

"I don't know, but I think the Camel got busted," I say, through coughs. "We have to get out of here."

"Out of here?" he questions. "We're in the desert, what do we do?"

"Just...collect any supplies you need. We have duffle bags in the back. Water, food, extra energy packs...I think we got about a day of emergency..." I spit blood onto the floor; I think I lost some teeth. "Day of emergency supplies...go pack now..."

He nods his head and flops out of his seat, crawling and then stumbling about the cabin, which is now full of displaced items.

I cling onto the chair and lift myself up. A pain goes through my knee, but I try to ignore it. What the hell happened?

In a daze, we go around the busted Camel, as smoke continues to clog the vehicle. We keep our heads down, grabbing as much supplies as we can and shoving them into makeshift bags. I gather all I can fit, and sling one onto my shoulder. It's a large brown bag that fits nicely wrapped around my back.

I look to Ulric, who is still trying to collect everything, but his hands are shaking too much to grasp onto the small packets of food and water. Migrating over, I help my distressed brother. Packing everything he'll need, and then handing him his armored helmet.

He looks at me with panicked eyes. I'm stressed as well, but I keep a still façade and maintain my composure, giving him an encouraging look and a pat, before placing my own helmet on with a satisfying, pressurized thunk.

The wind disappears, and all I can hear is my own breathing.

"Can you hear me?" I say to him through the short-range radio, pointing to my helmet.

"Yeah," he replies, followed by a cough.

"Alright," I say. "We need to get out of here."

"Where are we going?"

"To get help, same plan," I announce.

I open the back doors of the vehicle, and we flounder our way out. I trip, feeling myself traveling through the air before landing hard on my chest in a pile of fine sand. More pain, more heaving from the hit. It feels like I'm in a dream, surrounded by vivid, illuminating colors shining down on us from a large white sun.

A hand grasps my bicep and gives a tug. I situate myself on all fours and look around before regaining my step. The ground slips under my feet, and I struggle for a moment to maintain traction in the ever-shifting sand.

"What did we hit?" Ulric questions me through the radio. I look at him in his silver armor, now covered in sand.

I shake my head. "I don't know...."

We make our way slowly to the front of the smoking vehicle. The wheels rotate delicately in the air. A black, spread-out soot covers the front, along with more shattered glass. In front of it, there is a small crater. I know what we hit.

"It was a mine," I declare, pointing a finger at the crater. "Must have...must have been planted by the Scavengers that we battled."

"Why did it not blow us up?" Ulric asks.

I continue to cough, raising a finger for him to wait. The pain in my knee is not going away.

"Maybe...it was a smaller one...for treads," I theorize. "Not all of them are ship killers."

"Fuck," Ulric curses, "shouldn't we wait here? Wait for another Camel to come pick us up?"

"They won't send out another Camel for at least another day," I say. "And our armor only has energy for at a day, at most...I don't want to risk frying out here."

"So that means...," Ulric trails off.

"That means we have to walk. We're already so close to the Eagle Nest. I'd say forty or so kilometers. And we're about a two-day walk from the *Howling Dark*."

"So, I guess we walk then."

"I guess we do."

Temptation

Ulric and I wound our way across the hills and valleys of the desert, slipping and tumbling along the way. While on the ship, we cut through these sand dunes like anthills. Now we are at the mercy of them.

The cloth wrapped around me is doing its best to keep my body temperature down, yet sweat still migrates from my forehead down to my feet and everywhere in between. Welts have already formed, and we've only been walking for five hours. Luckily the sun has lowered in the sky, turning it a new hue of orange and purple. It will be sunset soon.

As we climb over another dune, I can see the lights of Eagle Nest #13 clearly. They turn on dot by dot across the tall towers, and the spotlights that shine on the buildings bring out the intricate details. We're close. We'll have to walk through the night, but we're close.

Throbbing guilt builds up slowly inside me like a tiny flame. It's a little voice that tells me this is all my fault. I should have listened to my brother and let him do his job. Those men who died in battle would still be alive. If we don't survive out here in the dunes, my mistake will have cost the lives of my brother and me as well. I dragged him into this. I knew what the Kiln was like, and instead of turning him away when he wanted to join me on the ship for a journey, I pushed away any doubt in my mind.

This land is for me, but it's not for him. I'd be willing to die, right here on top of this sandy hill, but I wouldn't wish the same fate on him. Ulric still has more to see, yet the Kiln offers nothing more. This is all it is—towers and sand, towers and sand. The first time I saw it, I was eager to see more, but that's all there was.

I was a fresh-faced kid, venturing out into the Kiln to serve my country. I didn't know what I'd see. I didn't know whether I'd die in that campaign.

"You say that I'm a savage," I suddenly say to Ulric through the radio. "But I've seen true savagery. I've seen what non-Aryans are truly capable of."

"You've told me this before, Ansel," he replies dismissively, while attempting to make his way down the dune.

"No," I say. "I didn't."

He gets to the bottom of the dune, turns around, and looks up at me, watching as I slowly slide down toward him.

"I was your age when I was first deployed," I say. "Eagle Nest #7 had been attacked by the largest fleet of Scavenger ships we'd seen since the Glass Wars. Came out of nowhere."

We march our way through the valley between two dunes, right in the middle of a long shadow from the evening sun.

"Whole Nest was overrun in a matter of hours. Any defenses were destroyed. The Scavengers, numbering in probably the thousands, just stormed the towers. They held those towers for at least a week before we were able to send in a reasonable force to stop them."

The wind dies down as the dunes block most of it. Sand cascades over the top like waves on the ocean.

"I was a new recruit. The only violent thing I'd ever seen in Germania was a squirrel being attacked by a dog. I didn't know what I was going to see."

We reach the bottom of the giant sand dune and begin our ascent. I need to crawl at times on my hands and knees to get proper traction and not slide back down.

"The initial assault was actually fairly simple. We sent in hovercraft and warships, knocked out any defenses they had outside. We were cheering as we cut down that green flag of theirs, burned it on the spot, and raised the swastika. Then we fought our way inside...."

I continue to climb my way up the dune.

"The Scavengers sent a group of civilians out as a defense, firing into the group and us as we entered the central tower. I saw an old man's skull split open from a rifle round. By the time the fire-fight was over, most of the group, women and children mainly, were bleeding on the floor. Some stayed behind to check for survivors. But I just kept going."

I reach the top of the dune, and look on at the towers.

"We cleared room after room. Bodies were everywhere when we entered. Girls were strung up on the walls. Men were gutted. The smell was just...something else. In the main hall, heads lined the walls."

"Ansel...."

"I lost my arm when we entered the next room. But it was that sight, the sight of all those civilians who lived their entire lives, had families, had everything destroyed because those greedy savages wanted to plunder. That was enough motivation for me to finish that fight, metal arm and all, and gun as many down as I could."

We stop for a moment and sit.

"You want to know why I want to keep the dams? Because the sea will just save them. They'll line the shores. They'll survive. I want all of them to burn in the desert. It might take a few hundred more years, but I know it will come one day. They will all be lost to the sand. And until that day comes, I will inflict as much pain on them as I can. I will never call a single Drop in my life, just so I can wrap my hands around every single one's neck, and squeeze."

We sit in silence for a moment. The wind and sand rush past us. My cloth rustles in the wind. The memories come flooding back. Those feelings of utter loss at the sight of bodies ripped apart by swords or bombs. Children disemboweled.

"If we didn't have the dams," Ulric begins, "then we wouldn't need to worry about any more civilians being killed."

"But we would have to worry about the Scavengers surviving."

"I'm sorry you had to see that, Ansel."

"Don't be—it opened my eyes to what awaits our people outside the Reich. You'll see it too, one day."

We walk the entire night without saying a word, simply trying to gain the most distance without the sun beating upon our backs. I cling onto my duffle bag, feeling the weight begin to make my back ache. My knee stings with every step. There's nothing I can do about it now. Best to just bear the pain. A pool of sweat has collected in my boots. Thin layers of liquid swash about with every step into the hot sand.

As I suppress the urge to sleep, I begin thinking that my mind has started to play tricks on me. The night sky dazzles and blurs. Our armor's flashlights appear to flicker.

My mind shuts off, focusing solely on keeping pace with my brother. It's odd how in these moments you can become aware of every action the body makes. I notice every breath I take, every blink I make, and every dry swallow, even though I'm so thirsty no saliva really travels down my throat. The intake of air into my helmet heaves in and out, giving me a fresh supply of cold, breathable oxygen.

I wonder if this is what the colonists on Mars feel like when they walk that Red Planet. The Kiln might as well be an entire planet by itself. For a while, I even become transfixed on Ulric's cape. The violet mast of cloth fluttering about in the wind, just like the flags from the bowsprit.

Eventually, the sky cracks with a burning paint of violet. The day has begun again in the Kiln, and the sun soon will shine down upon us.

"I'm sorry," I say to Ulric, who turns his head toward me, "I'm sorry that I got you into this mess."

"I knew what I was getting into," he responds in a calm voice. "It's the Kiln. I expected it to be dangerous."

"When we get back to the ship, I'll stop anybody from saying something to you about the Scavenger. If I had known earlier they were making you uncomfortable about it, I would have put a stop to it."

"How? You can't just order people to not be suspicious."

"True. But I could have done...something...we never should have had the Scavenger on the ship."

The sun appears to the east, casting our long shadows upon the winding hills. It graces the sides of the towers, creating a thin line of yellow light upon the tall, dark silhouettes. The towers' size is deceiving, making them seem closer than they truly are.

Light hugs around every sculpture, every face carved into its façade. They are as ornate as the monuments in Germania. Statues of Aryan warriors, depictions of past battles, and even past Führers scale the side of this endless pillar. Atop every tower are four eagle statues aligned in the cardinal directions. As I scan from top to bottom, the tower gradually grows wider like the steep slope of a mountain.

"It looks like the sand dunes end a little bit from here...we'll gather more distance when we have that flat land to walk on," I say, pointing in front of us. Out of the corner of my eye there is something that seems off about that dune. I turn to spot a large triangular object poking out of a sand dune to our right. The sunlight just barely shines upon it in a valley of shadows. It's a bright orange, a rusted orange that was only a shade brighter than the morning sand around it.

"What is that?" I ask, squinting down to the strange thing. Ulric turns to face where I'm examining.

"Do you think that could be a mine?" he says. "I don't exactly know what mines look like out here."

I squint my eyes and examine the rusted metal object. It doesn't look like any mine that I've ever seen, and I've dug up many over the last decade in the Kiln. All I respond with is a headshake. Before I can say anything, Ulric is sliding down eagerly to see what it is.

"Ulric, stop!" I yell after him, but I take a false step and tumble down the dune after him. My fall ends with a hard crunch, knocking the wind out of me. As I stumble to my feet, I can see he's already at the ship.

"Even if it isn't a mine...we don't know what it is," I say, catching my breath.

"It...it has a swastika," he announces, hesitantly.

I pause, and look at him with eyes wide. What did he just say? My legs drag me along toward the strange object, rejoining me with my far-too-excited brother. He points a trembling finger at a series of black lines painted just above the sand. Getting on his knees, he shovels away the dune. I can't believe it. A black swastika reveals itself, painted on the rusting metal of this thing.

"It isn't golden. Why isn't it golden?" Ulric asks. "Is it one of ours?"

"We need to keep moving," I say, knowing that we need to keep continuing toward the towers. My feet take me away from the strange object; yet after a half minute of walking I realize there are no footsteps behind me. Looking back, I see Ulric still at the object, his full attention on the swastika.

"I said we need to keep moving, Ulric," I bark louder, my patience wearing thin. Still no response. I yell his name louder.

"I heard you," Ulric says, his quiet voice coming through my radio. Sunlight fully extends into the valley. The cool break from the night air has ended, and I can feel the heat begin to beat down upon me again.

"Then, how about you stop staring at that thing and we keep moving?" I reason. Yet it falls on deaf ears as the armored Ulric crawls his way up the dune, getting a better vantage point on the object down below him.

"There's a hatch door," he analyzes.

"Stop it, it could be rigged with something, let's just—"

"It's a ship," he concludes.

I ignore what he says. "I don't care what it is, we need to go."

Yet before I can stop him, Ulric jumps off the dune, slinks himself onto the object, and lifts the hatch-door. My heart pounds as I anticipate it exploding, or setting fire, or something else at any

second. There is nothing except the sound of creaking old steel.
Ulric pulls out a gun and lowers himself down, disappearing under
the metal and sand.

I'm sick of him. If he wants to go exploring instead of helping the
ship, fine. I whirl myself around and begin climbing up a sand
dune, leaving the object in the valley behind me. As I continue
walking, I think about the promise I made to him, the invitation I
sent to him to come to the Kiln.

"Fuck," I mutter to myself, feeling the pangs of guilt. I stop dead
in my tracks atop the dune, the cogs turning inside my brain about
which path to take. After a minute, reluctantly, I dig my hands
into the sand and slide back down the dune toward the object.

I march to the ship and climb onto its rusted metal shell. My boots
hit it with a loud clang. The hole in the steel is large and circular.
A ladder leads down into a dark abyss. I take out my own gun as
well, not taking any chances this could be home to somebody else.

Putting two feet on the ladder, with each step I go lower into the
strange vessel, the echo ringing louder and louder. As I disembark,
I step onto a solid, yet aged, floor. There is no sand. No evidence
that this ship was in the desert. I guess the hatch-door did its job.

The flashlight from my armor shines into an open, hollow cave.
It's longer than it is tall.

"What are you doing?" I call out to Ulric. "We need to get out
of here."

"We needed a break anyway." His voice echoes through the
darkness.

My temper flares.

"We can take a break when we're actually at the towers."

"This cave just keeps going on, and on," he says, his voice getting
fainter. I can't see him through the darkness. As I shine a light
on the walls and floor, little details slowly reveal themselves
before me. Posters of proud-looking people. One has a man in a
brown uniform, with short blond hair. He's carrying a flag...with a

swastika, but it's nothing like the Reich flag. It's red, with a white center...and a black swastika. The writing is in German.

"The man on this poster looks like the Eternal Führer," I remark. "How old is this ship?"

"Is this not one of yours?" Ulric calls out in the distance, his own light shining around as he explores.

"This isn't anything like I've seen before. It...."

My eyes catch a glimpse of a series of papers on the wall. The top has a picture of a dog with brown, short fur, and at the bottom, there is a series of dates in a line. It's a calendar. The date in intricate letters reads, February 1960.

"This...this is certainly not one of our ships," I mutter, staring blankly at those big bold letters.

"Then what is it?" Ulric calls out somewhere in the dark.

"Something...far...far...older."

Dearest Emma

We've decided to rest inside of the ship's hull for long enough to eat and hydrate, since it's difficult to do so otherwise without risking sand blasting onto an unprotected face. We've taken our helmets off. The sand must have been blocking the heat from the sun, because it feels quite temperate inside those dusty walls.

I've told Ulric we're only going to stay for thirty minutes and then it will be out to walk again. Our flashlights have such a meager range, we're surrounded by emptiness. There appears to be lights above us, but I doubt this place has had power in millennia. Glass litters the floor and the crates that are stacked around the room. It must have been used for some kind of storage. We take our rest on some of the smaller boxes.

"This ship has been in the desert for thousands of years, then," Ulric says, taking a drink of water.

"I guess so," I respond.

"You'd imagine that in that time somebody would have found this ship by now," Ulric asks.

"Well, in the desert the sand dunes are like waves. It was probably just under the sand this entire time, and one day..." I make a whooshing noise with my free hand, "the wind just unburied this thing."

"Look at all of the artifacts in here," Ulric says giddily. "This is an incredible find. Imagine what sunk it."

"No idea, and frankly I don't really care," I state, motioning for him to leave.

"You're not even interested in what history this could hold?"

"I have priorities," I spit, taking another bite out of my packed food. "We have a ship to get help for. You took your break. Let's go." If I could stay here any longer I would. I need the rest. After sitting down for just a few minutes, my body now has had time to recognize the incredible pain in my knee. It's a slow-burning pain creeping down my leg.

Ulric puts down his food and looks around, his flashlight revealing every crack in the walls and the scattered remains of whoever went down with this ship. Skeletons lay curled up on the floor, some of them together. I wonder what their final moments were like as the ship sank into the sea.

"My entire life, I have been fascinated by the Reclamation, and now, I'm in probably one of the last remnants of it. I don't want to waste it."

"Fifteen minutes," I say angrily, "that's all I'll give you to look around, fifteen minutes."

Ulric's face contorts into a pleasant smile, and he begins searching around the hull, opening crates and rummaging through whatever is inside. I just sit, continuing to eat, dreading the moment I need to put pressure on my knee once again.

"Just think about it," he says. "These people lived during the time of Adolf Hitler. Imagine the world that they were a part of. The stories they must have told."

I look at a slumped-over skeleton directly opposite me. Its head is resting on a crate, a fine black coat tattered and sunken on his bones, his head slumped over his open jaw. It was quite a small thing. Guess the people were generally shorter back then before gene manipulation arose. Poor bastards.

The sound of falling papers and cluttering books fills the ship as Ulric explores every inch, like a child looking for sweets. This must be his candy shop. If this was any other situation, it would be mine as well.

"The Knights Historical Society would love this," Ulric gleefully says. "The flags look so different than our own. It's blood red. Strange. I never heard anything in the records about the flag changing. Do you think anybody knows? I wonder why they changed it. I think it looks alright. Maybe it was just one of the flags they had."

"Maybe."

More rummaging. More clanking.

"It seems like a lot of this is...personal objects. There are a lot of pictures. All the photos are in black and white," Ulric concludes.

His voice begins to fade away as my body gives out on me. I let my eyes rest for just a bit. The environment becomes a tad darker when I shut my lids.

"It doesn't seem like much of this was even really affected." Ulric speaks to nobody in particular. "No sand. No water. It's like a time capsule." I think he says a few more words before everything goes silent.

I awake with a jolt and instantly panic. How much time has passed? What has happened? Where's Ulric? I call out to him, and after a few seconds, he responds.

"You might want to see this," he mutters through the radio. I check the time, only two minutes have passed. I must have just blacked out.

"I really don't," I say, not wishing to leave this crate.

"No, I mean, you really need to. I found...something," Ulric insists.

Do I really want to play along with this? I could just not say anything and get my rest. Why do I tolerate Ulric doing this? I should just drag him out of this place. Then again, I really don't feel like dealing with an Ulric who is continuously talking about how we could have searched this ship more.

With a heave and an annoyed, deep breath, I lift myself off the crate and onto my knee, which wails out in protest. Maybe I really do need medicine. We packed some for the trip, and yet I couldn't find it when we fled the Camel.

As I lumber down the dark hallway, my light shines on a silver Ulric, who is leaning against a table, his hands flipping through documents.

"What is it?"

"I was looking through this skeleton's clothes, and it had these documents in his coat."

"What do they say?"

"Take a look, it's an older German but, it's still very readable."

My eyes scan the brown paper, the ink is a bit blotchy. I figure it's from water damage, however it's still somewhat legible.

> *Dearest Emma,*
>
> *The ship is going down. We do not know why. I think we were attacked. If I do not make it, I assure you my final thoughts were of you. Please do not mourn me. Keep up strong appearances for Moritz and Johanna's sake. You will be taken care of. I do not regret a moment of our life together.*
>
> *Love,*
> *Anton*

"Why is this important?" I ask Ulric.

Ulric takes the letter from me and looks over it.

"His coat had the same insignia as mine. Two S's...," Ulric says. "He was S.S."

"Wonder what brought the ship down. Was it a mine? An enemy ship?" My mind races with questions.

"I don't know. It's eerie. I'm going to continue looking," Ulric announces as he turns away into the darkness. His light shines upon a door, which he opens happily.

"Five minutes," I bark, followed by more "yeahs." Ulric disappears into the other room. I look over the letter again, while strolling around the crate-covered room. At my feet is the sprawled-out skeleton of a man in a brown shirt, much like the one on the poster. Across his boney arm is a loose black band that says S.S.– the same symbol on Ulric's armor. What was he doing on a ship that led him to die?

My curiosity now gets the best of me, and I go around examining the other skeletons. None of them have the same clothing as him. Some are small, petite...like children. Some are simply dressed in coats and hats. Civilians?

What is Ulric doing? I go through a small door and enter an even smaller corridor. More skeletons decorate the floor. Some brown shirts, other black shirts, many with civilian clothing. A gun lays next to one body. A rifle? I'm not sure, it looks tiny.

"Ulric?" I call, and my voice travels up the hallway, up the rickety stairs at the end of it.

"I'm up here," he says, "there are so many bodies. I think they were transporting..."

"Civilians. I know."

"No," he says, "I found another document. You should see it."

My metal boots take me up the unstable stairs, and I enter a small room. Sand covers the entire front of it, cascading and overflowing the small windows. This looks familiar. It's a Bridge...

"I went through one of the bodies. It had a large coat. This was in one of the pockets," Ulric says, handing the wrinkled note over to me:

> *For the safety of the European community, all persons of Jewish/Semitic origin have been advised to relocate to the island of Madagascar with cooperation by our French allies. All new governments express that it is in the best interest of the continent that both peoples separate. You will be paid and accommodated for your troubles. A Reich officer will be at your premises to escort you for further transport on the second Monday of March.*

"Are these bodies...Scavengers?" Ulric says, looking around at the confusing display. Skeletons lie about at the front of the deck, guns at their side. A mass of more bodies lie next to them, facing forward. Ulric hands me a locket.

"This was with the note."

I open it. The colored photo shows a small family. A mother, a father, and a daughter. All with pale skin, some noticeably foreign features, some not. Each has a yellow star on their jackets.

"Jews?" I say, confused.

"It says so," Ulric wonders. "But...Jews have dark brown skin. These notes were on many of them. And that yellow star thing is on all of the bodies as well."

"Odd," I say.

Ulric's attention turns away from me, and to the corner of the room. I look as well. There is a chest. A large wooden box emblazoned with a golden eagle, its wings outstretched. The two S symbols hang up above it. My brother slowly stalks toward it.

"We need to get going," I say, "exploring is over."

"Just, let me see this," Ulric asks quietly.

His hands run over the warped wood finish of dark oak. The gold, however, has maintained its elegant coat, even if it was just a bit dusty. With two flips of the hatches on either side, Ulric lifts the top of the chest.

"What about the *Howling Dark*?" I say sternly, whirling around. "We have to go."

Ulric says nothing. His head peers down into the box, arms still holding the top of the chest. After a slight pause, one of his hands reaches down inside. When it comes back out, it is grasping something—a large hardcover book.

"What is that?" I ask him.

"It's...*My Struggle*," Ulric mutters in a trance. "It says it's by Adolf Hitler."

"Well, you got another copy to your collection, let's go..."

Ulric says nothing again. He simply hunches over, looking down at the book, his back turned to me.

"But, he softly peeps, "that is not...Adolf Hitler."

"What are you talking about?"

He turns around and holds the cover of the book in my direction. My mind draws a blank, confronted with what I am seeing. There is no blond man there to greet me. Instead there's a sickly-looking man with dark hair.

"That's certainly not Adolf Hitler," I chuckle at the image plastered.

"It's not," Ulric mutters, lost in thought, flipping through the pages, "but it says it is."

Flame of Reason

Ulric and I stand there for a few seconds. His blonde head is curved down, poring over the cover of the book.

"You sure that says *My Struggle*?" I ask.

"Well, it does take up a fair amount of the cover," Ulric quietly replies.

I turn around and make my way to the small door. With one hand I motion for him to follow, yet he seems to be lost in his own world, transfixed on the book.

"The *Howling Dark* still needs our help, Ulric," I say to him in a calm voice. "We have to get moving."

"Yeah," Ulric says, not in a sarcastic tone like the other two times, but with a weight of agreement. He starts walking with me, holding the book in hand.

"You can't bring the book," I tell him.

"I'm not going to bring it to Europe, just…"

"Just nothing. I need your help and if you're going to be distracted by that thing…"

"I won't," he insists, snapping out of his soft-spoken demeanor. With one motion, he puts the book in a sack placed at his side. "Let's get going."

We navigate our way back past the skeletons, down the stairs, through the narrow hall, and into the open cargo room. The light from the sun shines directly through the hatch-door at the end of the dark tunnel.

"You alright?" I ask him.

"Yeah," he says with an unconvincing smile.

"My knee has been killing me since we left the Camel. What I suggest is you just forget about this place until we get our jobs done."

"Alright."

I place my helmet on my head, cold air rushes in, and I grasp the ladder. With each passing rung I can feel the temperature rising, even through the armor. The Kiln welcomes us back with a fiery embrace. My head pops out of the hatch-door, looking around to make sure nobody is staring down at us. I doubt there would be, but I'm paranoid.

As I get out of the ship, Ulric follows behind me. I lend a hand and help lift him out. We both stand level on top of the small space not covered in sand, left in a valley between two large dunes. The sun hasn't progressed much in the sky; it is still morning.

"Alright," I say, "let's go."

We crawl our way up and down the dunes. For about an hour, we say nothing. Surely he doesn't actually think that man was Hitler. We all know what the Eternal Führer looked like. Of course, as with anything during the Reclamation, there aren't actual photos of him; however, it's just common knowledge. His Aryan face is even engraved on the towers that we continue to walk toward. If anybody, an S.S. Knight surely could tell the difference. Just ridiculous to think otherwise.

I wonder how the *Howling Dark* is holding up. Volker knows what he is doing. I'm sure he's keeping the entire ship in check. All they have to do is keep the engines running, and we'll simply refuel at the Eagle Nest. This will be a small setback. An experience that Ulric and I will share. A very stressful bonding time.

Eventually, we reach the end of the dunes. The land opens up into flat terrain, easy to navigate and simple to walk. It's a relief for my feet and my body. Without the dunes to block the sand, however, the wind tries to force us back. I clutch my duffle bag tightly and attempt to barrel on through. It howls across my helmet. Wind and my own breathing—that is all I hear.

One step. Two step. Breath. The towers seem to get closer. Repeating for hours. The sun continues to rise. It's directly over us. More wind. Another step. Breath. Sharp pain across my leg. Wince. Look back to Ulric. Wind. Breath. Step. Swallow. Breath.

Ignore the calluses. Ignore the sweating. Look to Ulric. Step. Sun. Wind. Look to Ulric. I see him, his face down, the book in hand, and I stop.

"What are you doing?" I say to him, the wind screaming around us. My desert cloths are fluttering around, wrapping themselves around my tired body.

"I need answers," he mutters, not even looking up at me, not looking where he is going.

"Why?" I exclaim. "Is that face still bothering you?"

"I don't want to talk about it," Ulric says. "I want to just read through this. I don't know what is going on."

"You're a Knight. If anybody should be certain about who the Eternal Führer was, it's you."

"Exactly!" he yells, emotion finally escaping through. He stops in his tracks and closes the book, looking deep into the face that stares back. His entire posture is slumped, defeated almost.

"I...I should...be certain," he says. "It just doesn't make any sense. This book cover. This man. Who is he? Why does it show his picture?" He flips through the pages. "Three times, in three different angles. I saw some of his pictures in the ship too; that isn't coincidence."

"You're overthinking it," I brush him off.

"I'm really not. You're not even going to question—"

"No," I say sternly, cutting him off. "It isn't my place to question this. You need to throw that book away."

"I can't. I need answers," he stutters.

"Okay, here's an answer: That is not Hitler. You're welcome," I conclude, before turning around and continuing on my way.

"Then, who is it?" Ulric calls after me.

"Not Hitler."

"That's not good enough," Ulric says, his voice panicking. "You know those Scavengers didn't look like the Scavengers of today... what if that old man was actually telling the truth? What if he isn't a Jew?"

I laugh at the idea.

"That flag has changed...something changed in the Reich... something is off about all of this," Ulric says in a heavy voice.

"It's been two thousand years since the Reclamation. Of course things have changed."

"That's my point. Things aren't supposed to change. That face, that face of the blond Führer we all know, that was the man that made the Reich." He points toward the Eternal Führer's face engraved onto the towers of the Eagle Nest. "What if that face changed...just like the flag?"

"The desert is making you delusional," I say, attempting to ignore him.

"Ansel, you have not spent years of your life studying this. I have read over *My Struggle* countless times. Memorized passage after passage about what he has said. His viewpoints. Who he was. He was an Aryan, one of the few Aryans, and he created a Europe for people like him. That was the core of my understanding for this world." He babbles on, flipping through the pages before pausing, breathing heavily, and then saying, "And yet, when I read this, the words are different. Everything is different. The mindset. The tone of voice. It's like an entirely different person wrote this."

"Read more of it, and calm down."

"I have sacrificed everything for this. To study his philosophy. All scholars study his ideals. The Eternal Führer I knew called for peace among Europeans. Reconciliation after the war, even after Germany was punished. Among the ruins he planned to bring everyone together with Atlantropa. Yet..."

"Yet what?"

"Yet I don't see Atlantropa anywhere. No mention of it. There is living space...no...mention of living space on the sea, just east. That's all he says: east...." Ulric's voice gives up. "After seeing that Aryans can be savage, after seeing the flag, the posters, it makes... this book...seem fitting...fitting for something that we forgot about...or intentionally forgot...or changed...this isn't anything like the copy of *My Struggle* that I've studied."

"Shut the fuck up," I insist, turning around to block Ulric's path. I put a firm hand on his shoulder. "I have been walking this desert, I can't feel my feet, and am not in the mood for you to break down on me."

Ulric stands still; he says nothing.

"I told you, keep this inside. That meant, keep the book in that bag and don't worry about it until we get to fucking safety. I'm asking you, as my brother, to stop. Right now. Stop."

"Ansel, I...," he stutters.

"I brought you along because I was scared you would find some way to fuck up on the ship," I spit at Ulric. His mask stares back at me. He says nothing, so I continue on. "Maybe defend the Scavenger, say something stupid. And if you did, I wouldn't be there to save you."

"You brought me because you couldn't trust...me?" he says, confused.

"I don't know what is going on with you, Ulric," I say. "I was expecting a Knight who took no pity on the Scavengers. I wanted a brother who could support me when I punished those savages."

Ulric looks back at me, then to the book in his hand, then back at me again. We say nothing for a few moments. Two armored men in the middle of this flat dry wasteland...arguing over a book.

"This isn't a joke," I say, my tone becoming grim. "We do not have time to doubt the origins of the Reich. Doubt if the Führer was actually a black-haired inferior being. All that is expected of us is loyalty. Are you loyal?"

Ulric takes a few seconds to respond. Through the radio I can hear only stuttering. I repeat it again. Louder. Fiercer. He recoils back and nods his head in agreement.

"Good," I say, before turning around and continuing onward.

Fólkvangr

The idea of some sickly-looking, black-haired sub-human creating the Reich is laughable. Could a non-Aryan, a man who looked nothing like us, really be one of the founders of our entire race? That wouldn't make any sense. Why would somebody that wasn't one of us want to create us?

If anything, this entire thing was a misunderstanding. There is no reason to imagine that the man on the cover was Adolf Hitler himself. Perhaps it was just a warning. A symbol of a Jew? Something.

It's best to suppress this deep down inside. Yet it's very difficult to think of anything else while walking in this wasteland. As evening comes, we reach another series of sand dunes. They are smaller than the others and so instead of a long climb, it's simply an inconvenient incline from time to time. We are only two kilometers from Eagle Nest #13. Even from this distance, it takes up the entire world in front of us.

Eventually, as the sun begins to set, we crest over a large hill overlooking the entire nest. I can see a long cloud trailing away underneath the large metal walls. It's a ship. The wall makes even the largest vessels appear like beetles crawling around a simple staircase step. Sand flows like a wave across the kilometer of flat maintained desert, carried on by the wind until it clashes against the unmovable force of the steel barrier surrounding the complex of tall towers.

The walls are the best defense against a Scavenger attack. Sadly, however, sometimes they are not enough. The sides are as ornate as the towers. Memorials are metal-worked into the façade of great stories in Aryan history. The Glass Wars. The founding of the Eagle Nest. The creation of the Atlantropan dams. Atop the thick walls are a series of turrets, watchtowers, and tall flagpoles, each flying a display of gold and red.

"How much farther do we need to walk?" an exhausted Ulric asks.

"About another kilometer," I announce, my hands tightening around the straps on my duffle bag. Every step feels like needles

"Our ship went down and we request immediate assistance. We need a ship tow."

"Why are you not in a Camel, Captain Manafort?" she asks.

"We hit a mine. There wasn't enough time to walk back."

"We'll send out transport for you, wait right there," she says, before the radio goes silent.

Ulric looks at me.

"What did she say?" he asks.

"They're coming."

I take a happy breath before my knees give out and I flop down onto the soft sand as if it was a warm bed.

Just like earlier, I awake with a jolt and swing my head wildly to see where I am. I passed out again. I open my eyes and pull myself off of the ground. Ulric leans by my side with his hand on my shoulder. I ask him how long I was out.

"About thirty seconds," he says, his voice sounding as equally drained of emotion as mine.

"Guess I didn't know how tired I was." I chuckle it off, patting my hands across the front of my body, which is now caked in fine orange dust. The sand falls off and is carried by the wind.

As we look toward the series of tall ornate towers, I notice that one of the gates, a large archway with heavy steel doors, parts ways. It pushes away the sand around it as if it were merely kicking a small pile. If Ulric and I were closer, I imagine it would seem like a tidal wave rushing forward to envelop us both.

When the doors finish opening, something begins making its way through. The small ship that was making the cloud of smoke veers away as the behemoth emerges. A large gray beast migrates its way through the large gateway, just small enough to squeeze through the massive portal. It appears more like a moving island than an actual ship, and that's the point. That is how we are going to tow the *Howling Dark*.

are burrowing into my feet. My entire soles are covered in calluses. "That's when our short-range radios begin to work on their frequency. Or, if they spot us, that'd be nice too."

As we walk down the large, gradual hill that makes up the bowl that the complex is part of, I think back to the military. To when we came down a hill much like this, as artillery fire rained down on us. Back then, I couldn't imagine walking through that. Even in our vehicles it was catastrophic.

We asked why we couldn't all be put into hovercraft, but apparently the anti-aircraft fire was too much. Aegir Drops couldn't be used either, because it was our own city and we'd need to rebuild. So charging the Eagle Nest was the plan. Like the Knights of old, charging against a walled defense, one of my friends said. He died later that day.

Suddenly, the first crackle of radio fuzz fills my helmet speakers. My heart leaps. We're getting close. I can't feel the lower part of my body, or if I can, I'm certainly ignoring it. My tongue has become paper, scratching against the top of my dry mouth. It's been so long since I've had a drink of my water. Every attempt to take off my helmet has been met with the bitter blast of the intense summer heat. Every drink steals time that can be spent walking. It's not worth it.

The battery on my suit begins to flicker. We've just barely made it. Another half-day of walking and this armor would have given out. Ulric and I would have been cooked alive in our own armor. Yet for now I am met with the relief of a second voice crackling into my helmet, this one female, deeper than Ulric's.

"You are trespassing into Eagle Nest #13 territory, state your name or we will open fire," the woman states.

Even the threat fills me with joy; my legs almost give out, but by now I assume they are just used to the motion of going up and down.

"This is Captain Ansel Manafort of the *Howling Dark*," I say with bated breath, my heart pounding in my chest with every word.

"What is that?" Ulric says in amazement.

"That, Ulric, is a Fólkvangr," I declare in relief.

Ships breaking down or being damaged in the Kiln aren't rare occurrences. Since they are hulking bits of metal in the middle of the desert, it just isn't practical to try to fix them in the middle of a dangerous place. So, to remedy this problem, we have the Fólkvangr, a mechanical marvel at least three times the size of the *Howling Dark*. I would know, although I've only once had the chance to see one with my own eyes. It's more of a mobile city than anything else. A dock that comes to ships in need and transports them to safety.

The ship has no roof; in many ways it's shaped like a square bowl. In the center is where the damaged ship goes, and the Fólkvangr then brings it back to the Eagle Nest.

You would expect something so large to move slower than the average ship. It would just make sense. Instead, it can cover the same distance in a day as even the *Howling Dark*. It's quite a rarity to see one, and we're lucky that we broke down near a Nest that has one.

As it makes its way toward us, the sand beneath my feet begins to jitter and shake—millions of tiny particles all jumping around from the rumble of the Fólkvangr's treads. Thick clouds of black smoke erupt from its pipes like a volcano traveling across the desert sea.

Ulric and I simply stand in awe of the machine barreling toward us. The deep roar from its engines is deafening, even from a kilometer away. After a bit, Ulric simply decides to sit down, but I still stand. I need to keep up the appearance of a Captain, even if I did just trudge through the desert to get here. The roar becomes louder, shaking the ground and us along with it. Before we know it, it is upon us. Its exterior is more like a wall than a ship. Flags and banners fly from its edges, as if we were about to enter a small castle.

It soon blocks out the sun, casting a long dark shadow over us. The gargantuan machine stops not too far from us and lowers down a small ramp. Ulric and I trudge our way up the railed steel contraption, making our way toward a tall but thin doorway. The rumbling does not cease for a moment, so I hold onto the bars for support, or else I fear I'll tumble off into the sand below.

Grand Truths

This whole incident delayed our voyage by weeks. The sweat poured down my head every night as I struggled to fall asleep. Images of the Scavenger ship tearing holes into my faithful *Howling Dark* plagued my thoughts. Something deep inside told me that it was all because of me. Ulric was right. I really was too arrogant, confident that things would go perfectly. Another voice in my head tried to overpower the first. It struggled to tell me that there was nothing I could do, and that this was just an unlucky situation.

I know which voice was right, though, and that's why I had two weeks of sleepless nights. The best that came out of the situation is that the crew is alive and well. The cheers erupted like a stampede when I arrived back to the *Howling Dark* in the Fólkvagnr. The crew knew what it meant. It meant they were saved. The broken and contorted ship was slowly lifted inside the massive hull of the Fólkvagnr, broken tread and all.

That burning sensation of guilt waged war against my stomach as I saw such a lovely vessel dragged unceremoniously to be repaired. Apparently, we got there just in time. Volker explained that they sent a second Camel, but just a few hours later we arrived in the Fólkvagnr. If he and the rest of the crew blame me for the incident, they do a fantastic job of hiding it. I know that, in their position, I wouldn't have been so forgiving.

Every night I know that men died because of me and that I could have prevented it.

After a half-day of travel, the *Howling Dark* was brought to the docks of the Eagle's Nest for repair. The process to fix a broken tread is supposed to be "simple" but the steps are still slow and lengthy. This period of cooling down and "relaxation" only confronted me with all the mistakes that have led me here.

For two weeks, I frequently returned to see the ship being brought back into fighting trim. I tried to get at least some glimpse of progress. To see whether the tread was fixed, whether the glass was replaced. Maybe I wanted to relieve my guilt by seeing the ship getting fixed up. Maybe I came back so often because I was hoping they would say she was ready for us to get back underway.

The Eagle Nest was more than happy to accommodate the entire crew of the *Howling Dark* and fix up all our damage. They told me that we did a lot of good fighting with those two ships. Said there was no knowing what kind of damage they could have done to a smaller vessel.

We got a hero's welcome, if you will. A place to rest, a place where I could tend to my wounds. The crew was forgiving, the indoor city was welcoming, yet I knew that I didn't deserve any of it.

My knee healed up a bit: all it needed was some tending to by the Nest physicians. They told me that, after a week, I would be able to put some weight on it, to test it out and make sure that everything felt alright. So, I use this as an excuse to go for walks around the Nest. Maybe clear my brain.

I stand here in the central hub of the main Eagle Nest tower. Crowds of women, children, and men trying to get to work hurry around me. All of them have a place to be inside this massive cylindrical tower. Their footsteps clatter against the brown marble. The scene reminds me much more of a city square than the center of a building. There is no ceiling exactly. Instead, the tower is simply hollow, extending a thousand meters above my head.

As I peer up, I see bridges crisscrossing from one side of the tower to the other, the vital horizontal connections of this vertical city. Through these metal beams, rays of sunlight filter down from above, a reminder that the sun still is present here and that we still are in the Kiln, no matter how much the well-dressed civilians of this place attempt to think differently.

My knee begins hurting me again, so I decide to have a little rest next to an ancient stone fountain with statues carved in the likeness of the Eternal Führer and the original Aryans. They are the epicenter of this entire Nest complex. Beneath these gray figures is a pool of teal-blue water which flows around their feet, just like the crowd flowing around the fountain itself.

I glance at the statue, looking at the tablet in Adolf Hitler's hand. At the words engraved on it:

The Atlantropa Articles

"Quite the statue, isn't it?" a voice echoes behind me. I take my eyes of the plaque to see Ulric, looking nothing but disheartened. Bags have collected underneath his half-opened eyes. His beard has become disheveled and his hair unkempt. I'm hit with an immediate odor that warns me he hasn't had a proper bath in at least a couple of days.

"You're finally out of your room," I say to him, looking straight into his glazed-over eyes. He nods. After the ship was rescued, Ulric became a recluse, shutting himself off from the crew. The only time he appeared was when the ship had to be repaired and he moved his operations to one of the many rooms the Nest had set aside to accommodate us.

While others were out and about, drinking and whoring, he stayed in his room. Despite my best efforts knocking on that door every day, he would not answer.

"I've done a lot of thinking...and reading," he says, his voice struggling to maintain itself over the roar of the crowd. "I've done nothing but compare and contrast both versions of *My Struggle*. Two different versions of Hitler. What does it mean, Ansel, if this isn't true?" he points a hand to the central figure of the display. "If this depiction we have of the Führer as an actual Aryan...is just a myth?"

We both look at the towering Führer, his long stone robes flowing over and touching the tip of the fountain pool. In his left hand, he holds a document up high for all to see; chiseled onto it are those three famous words: "The Atlantropa Articles." His right hand, stretched confidently out at waist height, cups an eagle with majestically spread wings. The bird looks as though it is prepared to fly.

"You don't know it's a myth. You can't change your perception based on a single book. It was just a picture."

"There was more than one picture," Ulric says. "There are supposed pictures of Goebbels, Göring, Himmler...none of them...." He looks as though he is about to burst into tears. "None of them looked Aryan at all. They weren't like us...."

I raise my eyebrows, confused at what he was saying. "What are you getting at?"

Ulric sits down next to me on the bench in the center of this massive tower. We both looked out into the traffic of blonde, happy Aryans mindlessly making their way about on their day.

"They all had black hair, dark eyes," he chokes out. Reaching into his pocket, he takes out a couple of wrinkled old pictures and places them into my hands. I hold them before me, and my eyes go wide at what I see. My mind draws a blank.

There is the man in the old book: he looks short and stout, with his arm extended out toward the crowd in the same salute we do today. It most certainly looks like any rally we would have when I was a child in the capital. The entire crowd is signaling him. This was their Führer. There can be no other explanation. The same red-and-white flags hang behind him and the golden eagle as well. It feels so familiar...and yet...not. Like a dream where just the little aspects were off.

I look at another picture and see a group of unimpressive men dressed in brown uniforms. They look nothing like the Aryans of today. Dark hair, round bellies, and at the center is the same man again. All in the picture look at him with a sense of admiration.

My mind races, attempting to decide how to process this. I can't agree with Ulric. This is his livelihood. It would destroy him. I don't even know how to comprehend it. Is it a trick? Are these photos true? Not saying another word, I simply hand the pictures back to Ulric.

"So, what do you think of that?" Ulric asks me, his voice lined with desperation.

"I'm thinking that it could be anything," I lie.

Ulric scoffs at this idea. "Think about it. This is why...this is why we don't have records of the Reclamation...why we only have that depiction of Adolf Hitler," he points a shaking finger at the statue. "I have a theory...."

"Stop it," I say.

"I have a theory that, for some reason, the Reich over the years just shifted out what the Führer must have actually looked like for something that resembled the Aryans of today more.... I know that sounds...crazy. I don't know...it probably took generations... people might have just forgotten...."

"It does sound crazy," I say. "How would people just forget what the actual Führer looked like?"

"I don't know," he mutters. "How can people forget about that song? Sometimes, if something is lost, future generations will never know that something is missing in the first place."

He takes out the two copies of the book. The black haired man in the photo stares back at me with beady eyes. "Look," Ulric contemplates, scouring through the pages of the older book. "There is no mention of the dams in here. No talk about uniting Europe under the guiding hand of Aryans...there is...nothing that reflects our modern philosophy...protecting the tribe...."

"So?" I say.

"So. The entire Knighthood is based on this idea that the Führer brought everyone together in the name of peace. Europe built the Atlantropan dams, because of Aryan ingenuity, through our intellect in engineering and science. It was peace. But, instead, it just seems like he had other motives." Ulric's voice shakes as he blurts out each word. It is as if someone was stabbing him with every syllable.

I lean back on the bench and crane my neck up, looking at the empty center of this great tower. White light illuminates the entire structure with a mystifying glow. It is odd being in an area that isn't just sand and salt for once. I don't know if I really took the time to let that sink in yet.

"What does it matter?" I say to Ulric, who looks at me with an expression of confusion. "What does it matter if Hitler wasn't an Aryan like us? He still led the Reich. Still built the dams, and hell, led to this beautiful tower being built. Isn't that in itself a grand truth? The rest are just little lies."

Ulric runs a shaking hand through his messy hair, eyes bulging at the idea. This entire situation was truly breaking him. It was as if he was carrying a large stone and struggling to keep it from crushing him.

"It isn't just little lies," he argues, looking at particularly nobody. "This is the grand truth...What does it say about the entire state of the Reich if it maintains itself off of a false idea? The dams themselves were built by those men...the Kiln...All of the savagery that took place was because of those dark-haired men...non-Aryans...Don't you see we are just products of some inferior's plans that has lasted for thousands of years?"

"I refuse to believe that," I scoff, feeling my stomach churn inside at the very idea.

"But what if it's true? Ansel, I study this for a living...this book and these pictures should not exist. Ulric puts his face into his hands and breathes deeply, "I have no explanation for any of this."

I look at the old book. My eyes analyze every bit of it. An idea comes to my mind.

"How come that book survived the boat sinking?" I ask him, my hand reaching for the book. I flip through the pages. "Why are none of the words ruined or the pictures blurry?"

Ulric takes his face from his hands and skims through the pages. "It was in a sealed container..." he says, "no water was able to get inside..."

I say nothing, reaching the end of the book and turning back to the front cover.

"I see," I mumble, my mind going blank. As if on a reflex, or as if something else has taken control of my body, I lift myself off the bench with the book in hand. Ulric's face darts up to see what I am doing. My eyes glance down at the book, then at the fountain and the cool water running through it.

Ignoring the protests of my brother, I take the book with one hand and dunk it into the water in the fountain. A force presses against my body and I tumble to the marble floor. Ulric stands over me with arms outstretched as he lunges into the fountain. As he stands back up, he is holding the soggy book. A series of "whys" tumble from his mouth as he flips through the wet pages.

I pull myself back up, regaining my feet. He stares daggers at me. I look back at him without expression, dusting myself off. It seemed only a few people in the crowd turned their heads at the scuffle.

"Why…" Ulric mutters, "you ruined it."

"It wasn't healthy," I state, "you were becoming obsessive. It was destroying you. I should have burned it, or ruined it earlier."

Ulric paces around, cradling the book as if it was some dead child. His breathing becomes sporadic and his shoulders heave up and down. A hand goes to his forehead as he occasionally glances back at me.

"How can you not want to investigate this more?" Ulric spits. "Something is off, and you just choose to—what—ignore it?"

"Yes," I flatly state. Ulric stops, mouth agape. I dust myself off again before looking back at his wide-open eyes. "Nothing will change from this, Ulric. This world—is what it is. That," I point a hand to the statue, "is what made the Reich. Made you. Made me. Made the entire Kiln. I'm not going to be easily swayed by a few pictures."

I take the doubt that manifests inside my body and shove it deep down. There is probably some other explanation for all of this. Ulric is just ecstatic—that's all. The book isn't healthy. None of this is healthy. I don't need to deal with it right now.

"But...but I need answers," Ulric says. "How can I be a Knight if I'm not even sure in a tenet that I believe. If I don't even know who the Führer was? If I've been reading the wrong book my entire life? I don't even know if Adolf Hitler wrote this version of *My Struggle*." He holds up the book copy with the blond depiction. "The philosophies, the style of writing is entirely different..."

"Then, serve the philosophy of that book," I say. "The Reich of today is all that matters."

"He was bitter...that's all I got out of it...Germany lost the war. Yet, instead of rising from the ashes to embrace former enemies like the entire story goes, he actually just wished to win another war against them.... All I can think of is that the dams weren't his first choice, Ulric mumbles on, his voice becoming weaker. "And... and somehow he didn't go to war, I don't know why...instead, he decided to build the dams. Maybe he knew that war wouldn't work. Maybe the dams were a threat."

"We live in peace. Isn't that what matters? Our race still prospers," I state.

"Is this prospering?" Ulric says, looking at the wet book. "We drained the sea, Ansel. We fight against raiders in the desert. We've been told our entire lives that it was a part of the original Aryan's plans, but the more time I spend down here, the less use I see for this place. I used to tell myself it was worth it because it was written in the book. But I've spent my life studying a book that was written by somebody else."

"You will get back onto the ship and we will carry on as usual," I order.

Ulric chuckles and puts his hand to his head again. "If people knew what the Führer was really like, they'd want to reflood this entire basin in a heartbeat. We were duped. I knew there was something off about this place."

"The dams are the only thing keeping the Reich alive. For as long as they've been around, we've been at peace."

"You don't really believe that. You just want to stay in the Kiln," Ulric says.

"I'm done discussing this," I state. "When the ship is fixed up, you will get back on it. Then, if you want to ruin your life over this, go ahead."

"I'm only getting back on the ship to interrogate that old man. I still need answers whether you want them or not," he states. And with that, Ulric turns around and disappears into the crowd.

I'm left alone, sitting next to the fountain. There has to be some explanation for the book. Some reason for the red-and-white flag, instead of our red-and-gold. It's one of those thoughts you know is ridiculous to consider. What is the point? It isn't my place to worry about this.

Ulric doesn't realize that even answers won't satisfy him. They will only leave him empty. Wondering about what this place really is...I know what it is. It's the Kiln. It doesn't matter whether this place was created by a blond Aryan or not. I don't care. It doesn't change that people still live here and they need supplies. Ships still attack people in the desert.

This whole situation with the book could easily be the Scavengers' doing for all we know. Perhaps they did plant it—we don't know. That would make more sense than our Reich having a made-up depiction of our fucking Founder. My mind has no confidence in this assumption, though. I can't find confidence about many things anymore. There's just numbness.

Solutions

We are leaving the Eagle Nest early this morning. The treads turn once more, and the horn bellows a final goodbye to the people who helped us. That great stone tower casts a great shadow above us. I had gotten used to the cool artificial air of the city. As the massive gates open, we sail between them and out into the desert. Beyond the grasp of the shadow of our Nest, the heat returns in full force. Even through our own cooling systems, I can still feel it. The white, blinding sun greets us once again.

I was worried Ulric wasn't going to show, but he did, walking onto the deck with his head held low. We haven't spoken since the argument. There isn't much that needs to be said. What more can you say to a man who now shares a different perspective on this place, the Reich's origins, and the original Führer himself? You can't say much. You simply prevent him from foolishly spreading the words to others.

More sleepless nights haunt me. Guilt over it all. Getting the *Howling Dark* back into operation had given me no relief. The memories of our dead men still flash through my mind, as I toss and turn without relief. If I just didn't make that maneuver, we would be at Eagle Nest #18 by now, and my men would not have died. Ulric would never have discovered that damned book. My brother wouldn't be having some kind of mental breakdown. This is all my fault, and I know it. That voice keeps whispering into my ear every night. As a captain, I had a solemn obligation to protect my crew, and as a brother, I had a sacred obligation to protect my blood. I failed at both.

Some Aryan I truly am.

I stand on the Bridge of the *Howling Dark*, my arms held at my sides. The glass has been replaced, and the floor swept. My cigar dangles out of the side of my mouth, now reduced to a small, glowing bud of smoldering distraction. I pay it no mind, even as its falling ashes begin to kiss my cheek. I think I've smoked about five today, and it's not even noon.

The crew on deck go about their duties, and the engine continues its usual hum. Volker stands at my side, checking over the dashboard. He makes idle chat while we go about our business. My responses to him are short. Much is on my mind.

Volker stands next to me, looking over the charts. We have maintained a relative silence between us, ever since Ulric and I set off in that ill-fated Camel—ever since I saw him give that farewell salute...my First Officer, ready to go down with the *Howling Dark* in the place of its departing Captain. The normal order now restored, I have been tending to my own duties, and he to his own. Eventually, one of the things he says registers in my mind.

"So, where is your brother?" he asks in a casual manner. "He hasn't come up to the Bridge all day."

I pause, putting out the cigar butt in an ashtray.

"He's been keeping to himself lately. I think the journey through the desert just tired him out," I lie, focusing my attention on the buttons of the dashboard.

Volker nods his head in understanding.

"That was a pretty bold move of you to go and venture out into the Kiln, sir," Volker tells me. "Not many captains would do that. The crew appreciated it."

"I didn't do it for the crew," I say, the guilt coming back to me. "It was my order. So it was fitting that I go out."

There is a lull in the conversation. I take another cigar out from my pouch. Luckily, I was able to refill my supply at the Eagle Nest. I bought around thirty for the journey.

"Don't knock yourself up over it. The crew doesn't blame you," Volker reassures me. "In fact, if they think anybody is to blame, it's the Scavenger."

I pause, as the lighter stands still in front of my cigar. My mind goes numb, attempting to process what he just said. A chill goes through the cabin. Volker, realizing he just said something wrong, drops his head back down to the dashboard.

"What did you say?" I mutter, turning my head to Volker.

He looks up, his face in a grimace. "It's just a dumb rumor, sir," he says, attempting to brush it off. "I wouldn't get too worked up over it."

"Rumors are the news of the Kiln, Volker," I say, my voice becoming dull and precise. I make my way toward him with cigar in mouth staring directly at the uncomfortable First Officer. "What did they say?"

"They think he intentionally didn't call in the Aegir Drop, he admits.

"Why didn't you tell me this earlier?" I spit, my eyes glaring back at him. I couldn't believe what I was hearing.

"It's not like the men would do anything," he says, raising his hands up. "He's your brother."

"He was talking about how the men were giving him odd looks. How the fuck did this rumor begin?" I growl, my body leaning over his. Volker looks at me with worry, as if he would rather be anywhere else. The engine still hums.

"He was talking to that Scavenger all the time," he admits. "You know how they are. They try to connect the dots...."

My hand goes to my brow as I walk away. "I never should have let him keep that old man."

Volker says nothing.

"Why didn't you tell me?!" I yell, my arms flying up into the air. I almost drop the cigar. Volker takes a few steps back.

"You left immediately after the Drop. The rumors didn't begin until you were already gone."

"No," I say, smoke coming from my mouth. "Why didn't you tell me they were suspicious over the Scavenger. I would have just had him kill the fucker before any of this trouble started."

"It was mostly just suspicion," he says. "It wasn't really dangerous."

"Suspicion is always dangerous down here," I say.

Suddenly, it was like a calm had come over my body. One decision pops into my mind. A remedy to resolve this entire situation.

"He needs to kill the Scavenger," I say. "That's the only way he'll win back their trust." I say this but, in my head, I know this is the only way he'll win back my trust. I don't know what has happened to my own brother. He's changed. It's my fault that he's changed. I need to fix this.

"Alright, sir," Volker agrees.

My heart drums inside my chest. This is the only way. I don't know what that old man said to him. I wasn't down there to hear every one of their jailhouse talks. Perhaps he said something? Did I allow a Scavenger to infect my brother's mind? That was when he started talking ill of the Kiln. He saw me as a savage. It all makes sense now. I let the smoke out of my mouth and it climbs to the ceiling above.

"It's the best shot we have," I mutter, looking down to the deck below.

With every step, I hear the clang of my feet against metal. *Clank. Clank. Clank.* With every step I take, the tempo quickens. I make my way down the winding stairs of the tower and go underneath the deck. Strolling through the cramped corridors, I make my way to Ulric's room. My fist clangs against the metal three times. I wait. No answer. I bang against the door three more times. More waiting. There is no answer.

As I stride down the hall again, I go down another flight of steps. The sound of sand splashing against the bottom of the ship fills the corridor. Voices radiate across the hall. They become louder. When I turn the corner, I see Ulric once again in a chair with that damned book in hand, talking to the old man. His head spins toward me. I don't say a word and walk over to him, turning my attention to the Scavenger. My hand collides with the side of his bearded face and he crumples against the wall.

Ulric yells, standing up and lunging at me. I shake him off, pressing him against the iron bars. As I turn around, I see him staring at me with open eyes.

"They suspect you," I whisper to him. Ulric's shocked face falls; he looks down to the old man who is picking himself back up.

"Who?" he asks.

"The crew."

"About what?"

I let him go, and exit the iron cell. I take a puff of the cigar and smoke floats about the dimly lit room. "They suspect for some reason that you intentionally didn't call in the Aegir Drop."

Ulric lets out a laugh at the idea. "You were the only one who didn't want me to call in the Aegir Drop."

"I know."

"And so, because of your mistake, I am getting blamed?" he argues, laughing even more. "What a great situation. Thank you, Ansel."

"You were the one who wanted to keep the Jew. They wouldn't be suspicious of you in the first place if you hadn't been having these private chats with this old man," I spit, pointing an armored finger at the prisoner.

Ulric sits down. I pull up a chair and sit down with him as well.

"I don't know what is going on with you, Ulric," I say.

"What do you care about, Ansel...?" he says, staring right through me, his eyes glazing over.

"What is that supposed to mean?" I mutter, looking at him.

"I cared about being a part of a nation that was founded under the ideal of peace. A nation so intelligent and cultured that it spread across a continent and united lesser people. Eventually just...

absorbing them. Letting them all become Aryan," he whispers
to himself.

"When I lived in Germania there was a sense that I was a part of
something special. The great domes and the mossy pillars held
an awareness of history. It all did. I wanted to help preserve
that culture. I joined the Knights. Paid my dues, serving in the
Kiln...I thought that this place wouldn't be much different than
Germania...that the Reich could do no wrong."

We sit in silence. The old man shifts uncomfortably.

"Then I saw you break that girl's arm. I saw you smash that
Jew's face in, how you ignored me...just so you could serve some
vendetta against them," he mutters.

"Wait a minute—" I say, but he cuts me off, wanting to finish. My
fists clench.

"I started thinking about what the point of the Kiln even was...why
would we keep such a place that transforms normal Aryans into
men who commit such acts...."

"Because they are Jews. They have always..."

"They...aren't...Jews," Ulric says, pointing at the old man, "You
know why I've been interrogating him? Something didn't sit right
with me. Ever since he showed me that cross and that book."

"He's lying to you, and you're a fool to believe him," I say, losing
my patience.

"It wasn't what he said," Ulric admits, his voice lowering. "It was
what I found in that ship." Ulric takes out a picture from his
pocket. It was the image of the family, each with a star on their
chest that said *Jew*. "Those people that attacked us on their ships
aren't the people that we banished during the Reclamation. They
look different. They are darker skinned. They aren't Jews."

Ulric points to the cross on the old man's neck, "It can't be a
coincidence that he has the same symbol that I do. Do you think
the Reich would just adopt a Jew image? No. In our discussions,
he has kept repeating the same things...that we lost our way. That

we used to follow the same faith as him. And through that book you destroyed, the old *My Struggle*, I found out what it was. The Führer criticized it. It was something called Christianity."

I lean back in my chair, looking on at my brother in disgust.

"He is a Christian, not a Jew," he concludes. "And by what he's said, the Kiln is the only reason why there are attacks on Aryans at all. It destroyed everything down south, and so they raid our people. Can't you see how counterproductive it is?"

I take another puff from my cigar, smoke covering up my brother's worried face. I close my eyes. "You are going to execute him in two days," I flatly state, leaning out of my chair and standing up.

Ulric shakes his head in disagreement. "I can't do that, Ansel," he mutters. "There is still so much I don't know. I need answers."

"No you don't," I state. "You need the crew off your back. You need to show me that I can still trust you."

Ulric looks back at me, still sitting in his chair. A chill goes through the room. The constant sound of gravel smacking below us continues on. The engine hums.

"And if I don't?" he asks, glaring at me.

"You will," I mutter, looking back at him without any emotion. It was like I was looking at a hollowed-out version of somebody I once knew. "I need to know that you haven't been compromised. That you're still loyal."

"To you?" he says.

"To the Reich," I say. We look at each other.

"Like you care about loyalty to the Reich," he says.

"You need to show that you are not going to be an issue for this crew or me," I say. "If you're loyal to the ship, you're loyal to the Reich."

"If you cared about what was best for the Reich, you'd know that I'm not losing my mind. You'd know I just want to get to the bottom of whatever is going on here. How can I serve something that's based on a lie or a myth?"

"You can, because you will," I say. "This isn't a negotiable option. I'm trying to help you, you idiot. If the crew thinks you are a threat, they will do something. They've done horrible things to traitors before."

"So, I'm a traitor now," Ulric says.

"That is your choice."

Ulric pauses, looks at the old man, and then puts his head into his hands, cursing underneath his breath. I continue looking at him, listening in case I hear footsteps. Nobody ever comes down to this part of the ship, but I should still be careful.

"If I do this, you know that it won't be over. After this journey, I will still try to find answers," he says. "Something is off."

"I don't care if you do," I say. "Just put on a good show. Do your job, and let me continue with my own. If you want to ruin your own life with this fantasy, then that is fine by me."

"You saw the pictures, Ansel."

"I did."

"And you won't even question them?"

"It's not my job to. The Kiln has been good to me. The Reich has been good to me," I state, standing and putting the chair up against the wall. "I know my place. Now learn yours."

Redemption

The sky is painted orange with just a hint of deep violet, so the crew is probably stirring belowdecks, anticipating today's event. For the last two days word had spread about my brother's upcoming execution of the Jew.

As I stand on the deck, more and more men begin to trickle onto the front of the ship.

"You must feel pretty excited, this being his first execution!" First Engineer Keller tells me, his helmet covering up his normally greasy face.

I nod in agreement, but secretly my stomach twists around. Even through the greetings and saluting, I can't help but feel utterly betrayed by all of them. Can I really blame them, though? If I was in their place and another man was so willing to entertain a Jew, wouldn't I be suspicious of him as well? Being stuck in the middle of the desert can make men do unthinkable actions when they believe they are in danger—when they believe they are among enemies. This an environment that breeds suspicion, I suppose.

Fuck Ulric for putting me in this position. Fuck me for letting him.

The announcement that the execution would begin soon blared out ten minutes ago. I sent down some guards to bring the old man up here. They should be arriving any minute, and so should Ulric. I wait, hoping to see the crowd part for the violet-caped Knight.

Since there's not much wind, I can hear the rumbling of the treads. As I look back from the front of the ship toward the scorched desert plain behind us, I see the usual large cloud of sand floating gently in the wake of the *Howling Dark*. I hold my hands behind me, pistol strapped against my chest. My back faces the distant cliffs of Africa, which are rising slowly as the ship growls ever-onward in their direction. We are almost at the edge of the Kiln.

A series of towers stands in the distance, their image blurry in the rippling heat of the desert. Our destination, Eagle Nest #18, is in sight. But for now, we have more important matters to attend to. Ulric needs to show his loyalty.

Just to make sure he will actually show up, I decide to walk through the crowd, going belowdecks. After a brisk walk through the officer quarters, I knock on the door. Without a wait, it swings open and before me is Ulric, glorious in his full armor. The metal has been cleaned and glimmers golden-brown. His expression, however, is anything but glimmering. He looks back at me with eyes full of contempt.

"It'll be fine," I counsel, putting my hand to his shoulder. "Just say your lines, pronounce judgement on the old man, and then end it. It'll be quick."

"I know," he says quietly, putting his helmet on top of his skinny face. He hands me the old copy of *My Struggle* before I can say anything. He continues on, and I follow.

As we step up onto the deck, we see the entire crew standing around us, eager to watch what is about to unfold. With our helmets donned, we stroll through the crowd. Everyone steps back to let us pass. As we reach the tip of the bow, I see that the old man has already been brought up. He is being held up by two guards who grasp him by his frail arms. His eyes are closed, as the sand from the wind clashes against his eyes.

Cheers and clapping rise like a wave among the sailors as we approach. I raise my arm and put it back down. The guards comply, throwing the man to the floor with a solid thunk. He looks about with eyes covered, shielding himself from the particles. With mouth agape, he takes in the mob around him. This deck is colored a faded red, a remnant of the execution from his comrades.

Ulric pauses for just a second before I grasp him by the arm and lead him forward. We pass the shivering old man and turn toward the joyous crowd.

"Gentlemen," I announce in a raised, yet calm demeanor. "As you know, my brother, S.S. Knight Manafort, a few days ago requested of me that we keep one of the Scavengers as a captive." I point a hand to the curled up man. "Now, my brother has informed me that the man has given him all he needs to know. He is no longer of any use to this ship, nor to the Reich," I continue.

The Scavenger's face shifts around as he recognizes the words I'm speaking. His expression changes from confusion to realization. His brown features turn to face my brother, whose face is covered in his armor. Ulric simply keeps his composure, not saying a word.

"But...we talked...you," the Scavenger whispers to my brother, starting to raise himself from the deck.

"Quiet," I order, kicking the prisoner's head with my metal boot. The old man crumples back down onto his belly, and holds his wrinkled hand to a bleeding forehead.

"Ulric." I turn to face him. My brother's posture is rigid and his arms are held at his sides. I take my pistol out from its holster, Ulric reaches out his right arm, and I hand the gun to him. His helmet, with its glowing visor, turns toward me and I take one long step back, giving him space. Ulric looks down at the weapon, then at the old man, then at me. I give a single nod.

"This Scavenger," Ulric begins, his voice full of uncertainty, "has spoken a lot about his homeland, and his people to me in the last few days. As a scholar, I have collected valuable information on how the Scavenger mind thinks..." he pauses, "and how it contorts."

Ulric turns around to me, and raises a hand toward me.

"I am grateful that my brother has allowed me to perform my studies on such a rare subject, and I'm glad you are all here to witness me take my next step...as a Knight."

The old man situates himself and kneels at Ulric's feet. Dirty hands move under his draping silver cloak, and he raises up the necklace with the cross, grasping it tightly in both hands. It glints in the morning sun as he holds it up in his shaking fists. Ulric looks at me, and I give him a slight nod. With this, he kicks the man, sending him back to the floor, outstretched. Laughter erupts from the crowd. It's working.

"When the Eternal Führer envisioned the Atlantropa Dams, it was to bring peace and stability to Europe. To our tribe. But that was only the first part. The original Aryans knew that, as long as the Scavengers stayed, our minds would be corrupted by their influence. Brother would turn against brother," he turns his head slightly toward me, with a pause. "War would remain."

"But studying this...Scavenger...is a lesson for us all. A representation of what the Eternal Führer had to deal with in his day...what he was up against. We are lucky today to live in a better age because of that struggle.... We do not need to deal with the Scavenger threat anymore, except for in the desert...and we do not need to deal with this Scavenger anymore."

Clapping permeates the air around me, as the crew raises their weapons into the air. The old man is mumbling to himself, his eyes closed, hands held to his chest. He is calm. Calm, like the last Scavenger I tossed over the side of the ship. His face is relaxed, even as Ulric looms over him, holding his pistol to the man's forehead.

"So I am going to execute this Scavenger, in the ways of the old Aryans, with a pistol, and some words," Ulric mutters, still looking at the old man.

Ulric chants: "I light my path with the flame of reason—"

The Scavenger puts his hands to his necklace, running his fingers over its engraved carvings.

"I warm my heart with the pride of race—"

Chanting and hollering are rising among the crew. I look up and see Volker looking down from the tower Bridge balcony. The golden flag of the Reich waves elegantly above him.

"I love my Führer for all Eternal—"

The old man opens his eyes and gazes at Ulric. His lips form some words—I can't hear what they are, as the chanting drowns them out. Through the noise, I hear Ulric declare:

"For his life is what gave me grace."

I wait to hear the gunshot. To confirm that all of this will be alright. Yet there is a pause. Ulric just stands there, his gun still held to the forehead of the Scavenger, who looks at him, unmoving. Only the wind makes noise. Sand rustles across the steel deck. Everyone is silent. Everything is still.

The crowd watches on as a minute goes by, two minutes, Ulric's gun glimmers in the sun, ready to shoot point-blank into to the old man's skull. Inside I am screaming, begging for him to do something, to show the entire ship that he is a loyal Aryan. *What is he doing?*

He looks back at me, and I look at him. We are only meters apart, yet it feels like it may as well be kilometers. The gun, to my horror, starts moving downward as Ulric lowers his arm and his helmet begins to bend forward and down, following the gun. The gun is now perpendicular to the steel deck. My brother's helmet is parallel to the darkening horizon, but his visor gazes down onto the old man's upturned face.

He didn't shoot. *Why the fuck didn't he shoot? Why would my own brother refuse to shoot that creature?* I look on, feeling like a passenger in my own body. The emotion, the nervousness, the stress my brother is causing me...it all disappears. His traitorous words begin to ring inside my skull. Everything he said about the Führer, about the Kiln, about me. My brother...is gone.

I thought I could save him, yet he's been corrupted. His ideology—even who he was, has vanished over the last few weeks. *I did this to you, Ulric.* I never should have invited him. Shouldn't have given him the benefit of the doubt that he'd succeed in the Kiln. Instead, he despised it. I look on at my brother as he stares back at me.

Yet another voice goes through my head. He was the one who let himself be influenced by the lies. Weak in that sense.

Angry chants blast through the air, as many begin to call for Ulric's head. I look on, as if I was in a dream. Bodies begin throwing themselves at my brother. He raises his arm. There's a bang. Light permeates from his pistol as one armored crewmen collapses to the ground.

More chanting. I just stand there. I feel...nothing. Ulric failed me. He failed the ship. He failed the Reich. There is no more worrying that he will do the right thing. This is perhaps just who he is—a coward. As he looks back to me, more men lunge at him.

Volker comments something on the radio, something about me stopping them, and yet I simply mutter, "It's okay."

With hands behind my back, I begin to stroll closer to the commotion. More gun shots ring out; someone lands at my feet, yet I continue on unflinchingly. Everything feels numb. He failed me.

He had so much potential and yet he squandered it.

I hear him cry out as he is hoisted into the air. Bodies flood about the deck as the entire crowd begins to move away from me. Some look back to their Captain, and yet all I do is raise my hand. I could stop this. I know I could. And yet I'm not. Why am I not?

A voice inside says that perhaps I'm just tired. Another says that this is for the best. The one screaming for me to save Ulric has been pushed down deep and locked up. As the crowd storms away with my brother in hand, they ignore the old man, still rolled into a ball on the deck.

As everyone disappears, all there is left is his shriveled body, the gun that Ulric dropped, and me. He looks at me and attempts to lunge for the gun. My boot goes down hard with a solid crunch. There is a yowl. He pulls back his arm which now bends at an unnatural angle. I think I see a bit of bone. I smile.

Calm and collected, I bend over and pick up the gun, checking inside to see how many bullets are left. Three. That's good.

As I look back, I expect to see the old man crawling away, yet instead he looks back at me with his arm to his chest. The pain in his eyes is tremendous, and yet he holds it in. We look to each other. He does not run.

Without another word spoken, I raise the pistol to his temple and pull the trigger. The round rips squarely into his forehead. A clean shot. The body instantly flops onto the deck, crumpled and defeated. The ring of the gunfire echoes throughout the empty desert.

I'm left with just a dead body for all my troubles. *Fuck him. Fuck me for allowing Ulric to keep him.*

I think my feet are moving, I feel my body going forward, its acceleration toward the crowd walking to the back of the ship. All else around me fades into darkness. I feel nothing.

Chanting permeates across the ship as bodies rush to the commotion. A crowd has swarmed around Ulric. He tries to kick, punch, yet a series of blows send him tumbling toward the deck as well.

Ulric calls out to me on the radio. I can hear the pain and fear in his voice. My body has no response to it. I feel nothing. He failed to do what he needed. He did nothing but criticize my domain. I did everything for him, but he decided to throw it all away on an old man's life.

The crowd reaches the edge of the ship. Glowing visors look back to me for guidance as I casually stroll across to the stern. When I reach the festivities, I am greeted with a cheer.

My brother struggles to get himself free. His limbs are held by guards and his violet cape is wrapped around his neck. My mind is blank seeing this image. *Is this what it has come to?*

"Ansel, Ulric chokes out in a panicked voice. He turns to me. The crowd goes silent as I face my brother.

"Ulric," I say, my voice laced with disappointment. I can feel the pain well up inside. I want to help him, I want to do everything to bring him back, but I know that he is lost. A battle rages inside me as punches and blows rain down on Ulric. His metal helmet clangs with each of the strikes, until eventually his helmet is knocked clean off and the crowd starts battering his unshielded face.

He looks at me, wide-eyed and bruised, one eye closed shut from the swelling. Blood trickles down from his mouth as he coughs violently.

"Why didn't you shoot him, Ulric?" I mutter to my brother. "I gave you every chance."

"He...he isn't a Jew...I don't know...," Ulric sputters out. "I couldn't do it."

Tears begin to stream down my face. My helmet conceals it. I tried everything to save him—or did I? Did I do enough to prevent him from going down this path?

I mutter, holding back my voice from cracking: "You knew this would happen and yet you still spared him."

"If I pulled that trigger, then the Kiln would have won. Would have changed me into all of you."

He keels over as I deliver an elbow into his stomach. The guards hold him back as the breath is knocked out of his body. My hand goes to his head, and I pull him close to my face. The tears stop.

"I could have saved you," I tell him. "Pulled you back from whatever manifested inside you and yet you didn't see."

"I did see," he says. "You saw too. You just chose to ignore it."

I stand back, looking on with no feeling, thought, or reaction to the scene in front of me—once again, I'm just a passenger in my own head. The crowd swarms over Ulric's wriggling body. The ropes come out. The knives come out.

"Aren't you going to do anything, sir?" Volker says to me.

"He lost his way," I mutter. "I can't do anything."

I turn my radio off as screams echo inside my helmet. The only sound that comes through now is the soft whistling of the wind. It overtakes all the noise. The chanting. The screaming. The wind, so familiar here in the Kiln, makes it all go away—it's almost relaxing. I cross my arms and take it all in, suppressing that voice deep inside,which is telling me to go and save him, to take him away from all of this.

The rope wraps around Ulric's legs. *You did this to him.* The knives come out. *You could have done something, but you didn't.*

Ulric wriggles about and more punches send him to the floor once again. *They are blaming him for your failings.* Ulric attempts to grab at the rope, but he is kicked away. *He chose to spare the Scavenger.* A boot kicks Ulric in the face; blood pours from his nose. *He ignored my advice in that abandoned, ancient, water-borne ship, and his curiosity led him to that damned book.* Ulric attempts to wipe the crimson fountain flowing from his face, but his hands are grabbed by a half-dozen men. *He brought this onto himself.*

The crowd turns to me, eager to hear what I have to say. Ulric squints at me. The sand is thick in the wind. I walk up to him and take off my own helmet. Our eyes meet. We say nothing.

"There will come a time when this desert will consume everyone in it," he gurgles, the blood oozing from his lips. "Even a fish can drown."

I don't say a word. My mouth stays clamped shut as Ulric is hoisted up by the crowd. Through the wind, I hear a soft yell as his body thrashes about. Cheering erupts as the skinny frame of the S.S. Knight goes tumbling off the edge of the ship into the cloud below.

I'm sorry, Ulric. I wanted what was best for you.

For Those Who Journey Into

I hold the old copy of *My Struggle* in my hands as I gaze out from the bow of the ship. I took the book from Ulric's room after his death. The face of the pathetic sub-human my brother called Adolf Hitler looks back into me accusingly. It is just a faded picture, just a face, just another thing out here in the Kiln. It has nothing to do with me, nothing to do with my life. How did Ulric become so engrossed by this image—so entranced by this so-called Hitler's hypnotic eyes that, in the end, his confusion and disgust killed him? As I look at the unfamiliar, black-haired portrait of the Reich's legendary Eternal Führer, I feel no will to search for answers. No questions arise in my mind about what it signifies.

Or, if I did indeed have any desire to know more, I have shoved that curiosity deep down inside me. So deep that I don't hear its voice—so deep that I can sleep again.

The towers of Eagle Nest #18 are in clear view. They rise over the desert in a magnificent display. The carvings of eagles, of the swastika, of our blond, Aryan Eternal Führer—all in full glory on this façade.

My brother is dead and I did nothing to stop it.

I look down at the book again. The book that drove him mad. The unblinking eyes of the man on the cover stare back at me. Do I dare open it? I hold it with two armored gloves, standing at the bow of the ship, high above the flat desert. As I turn the pages, I can see that bits of it have become blotchy from the water—still, much of the text remains legible.

What if this truly was the original *My Struggle*, written by the original Adolf Hitler? Would it matter if the contents of this book, and our view of this person, did indeed change somehow over the millennia? Does it matter to me? I stare blankly back at the pages, flipping through them mindlessly.

I killed my brother. That is a fact that I cannot escape now.

I don't think I really need to know what the book can tell me about Hitler, or about the history of the ancient Reich. I'm content not knowing why the Atlantropan dams were actually built. The effect of the dams has been that Europeans have not fought a war against one another for thousands of years. That's what I care about. I don't need to know who the real Hitler was, because the legacy of that name is enough to inspire millions to this very day. That legacy is what is most important.

The dunes roll far off onto the horizon. The engine still hums. *I led my brother to his death.*

As I look over the edge of the ship, I can see the sand part, blazing a trail across the deserted plain as the ever-turning treads carry the vessel along. Everything is quiet. I want everything to continue to be quiet. I'm tired of the noise. I'm tired of the fighting inside my head. Tired of this book. Tired of the Kiln.

I lean against the side of the ship and take out the lighter that I use for my cigars. The small flame licks at the bottom of the book and suddenly flashes up over the cover. Hitler's supposed face is engulfed by the small inferno. My gloves protect me from the heat and I hold the smoldering thing as it turns into a fireball.

Without a second thought I let go, watching the book fall to the desert floor—smiling to myself as it is churned up into the treads, becoming one with the sand.

Acknowledgments

This novel was my first step into writing. It was a process which took a great amount of energy and, most importantly, the attention to those closest to me. I cannot thank my family and friends enough for their support and patience.

My mother, Julie, has pushed me to do better in every aspect of life. Nobody else has inspired and supported me more than she. My mother has and always will be the person I hope to be. My brother, Tyler, bore through hours of conversations detailing the world of *Atlantropa* and helped shape the narrative from those talks. My father, Ken, gave some very keen insight as well.

To Izzy, my fiancée, I am forever grateful for the purpose she has given me. Without her by my side, I doubt I would have felt any sense of drive in the evolution of my channel and my career.

All who were involved in the actual development of this book, I have nothing but gratitude for. Joseph Pisenti was the one who brought my attention to Mango Publishing. Together, we fleshed out an early concept of the world which changed and shifted so much during development. The finished novel is only a sliver of the ideas that were discussed.

The wonderful people at Mango Publishing lit the path for me in this journey into writing. Managing Editor, Hugo Villabona, contributed to the flow and style of the narrative. His team has the best second opinion one could ask for.

My longtime friends, Caleb, Tyler, Riley, Phil, and Charlie introduced me to the worlds and stories which influenced this novel. Tristan and Tigerstar continue to stay my greatest friends online and I love discussing history with them. Thank you for putting up with my ramblings.

I thank my fantastic community who brought me every opportunity I have today. You're a group united by the love of history, the evolution of nations, and how all of these concepts influence our lives today. This novel could never have existed without your love of the alternate history genre.

Without the help from everyone along the way, I can theorize with certainty that I would have nothing in this timeline. Thank you all.

Cody Franklin

Cody Franklin is the creator behind the YouTube channel *AlternateHistoryHub*. As of the summer of 2018, the channel has amassed 1.5 million subscribers with over 150 million views.

The Atlantropa Articles is his first foray into fiction writing. The illustrations that follow are his original creations that depict his views of the characters in this world. Cody currently resides in Whitehouse, Ohio.